VOICE IN THE DARK

Judy Whitten

A KISMET® Romance

METEOR PUBLISHING CORPORATION
Bensalem, Pennsylvania

For Gary, with love.

JUDY WHITTEN

Books have always been a part of my life. For me, the love of reading and the urge to write seemed to develop simultaneously. As a child, I spent countless hours making up stories for my own amusement. That habit continued into adulthood until finally, with my husband's encouragement, I quit my "outside" job to devote my attention to writing full time. My family backed my decision one hundred percent, and they continue to be my primary source of support.

The plane shuddered violently before settling into a glide almost as smooth as before the vibrations had begun. Slowly, Rae let out the breath she hadn't realized she was holding and glanced at her sister's pale, terror-stricken face. Karen had never liked flying. This experience wouldn't lessen her anxiety.

"It'll be okay," Rae said with as much assurance as she could muster, reaching across to pat the hand that clutched her wrist so tightly it threatened to cut off her circulation.

Karen looked past her out the window, and her eyes widened with fear. "It's on fire." Her hoarse whisper magnified the eerie silence that had settled over the passenger cabin when the emergency had become apparent.

"I know," Rae answered softly, struggling to maintain her composure as her heart raced out of control and her throat constricted, making it difficult for her to breathe. With Karen so near panic, she didn't dare let her own fear show. "But pilots are trained for things like this. Besides, we're almost home."

Karen stared out the window, transfixed, as they continued their rapid, gut-wrenching descent. "Fast. Too fast. We won't get home." A strange calmness entered her voice. "Rae, whatever happens, take care of my little girls."

"Don't be silly. Nothing's going to happen." Following her sister's gaze, Rae turned in her seat to check their progress. The airport lay directly ahead, tantalizingly near, but Karen could be right. They might not make it. It would be close, and close only counted in horseshoes and grenades.

"The girls." Almost choking on a sob, Karen clutched Rae's arm with both hands. "Take care of them. Promise!"

"I promise." Quickly, she broke Karen's grip and pushed her head down into the crash position the flight attendant had shown them. "But we'll get through this. Stay down. As soon as we're on the ground, get out of your seat belt. Emergency exit's two rows forward. Got it?" She, too, bent over to protect herself. "Two rows, Karen. Remember!" A tremendous jolt rocked the aircraft as it made contact with the ground, and pandemonium erupted around Rae. Screams, cries, and curses blended with metal grating on metal and with other rending, thumping, grinding noises into a mind-shattering sound that went far beyond anything in her experience. The plane bounced once, then hit again with ever greater force, throwing Rae against the restraining seat belt as if she were a rag doll and collapsing the landing gear before careening to the left into a skid that lasted forever.

When it became possible to move, she unfastened her seat belt and scrambled to her feet, relieved to find Karen already standing beside her.

"Emergency door," she shouted, shoving Karen into the aisle. "Two rows up."

But in her haste to follow, Rae tripped. Losing her balance, she fell into the seat Karen had just vacated.

By the time she had struggled to stand back up, she'd lost contact with her sister.

Relying on instinct, Rae moved into the aisle. Immediately, she found herself surrounded by a pressing crowd of people, all desperate to escape the wreckage and the smoke that began to fill the cabin. Time stood still, each second magnified into an infinity. For all the movement around her, no one seemed to be going anywhere. This, surely, was hell. Had she died in the crash after all? Was she doomed to spend eternity amid a group of terrified strangers futilely seeking escape?

As if in answer to her horrifying speculation, the aisle in front of her suddenly cleared. At last she could move. But where to? She'd lost count of the rows of seats. The emergency doors might as well be welded shut for all the good they were to her. All her careful planning was useless now that she'd lost her bearings, and her mind refused to respond to the crisis. Panic seized her. Giving in to the need for movement of any kind, she began to run.

Gasping, choking on the dense, acrid fumes, eyes streaming, she ran blindly down the smoke-darkened aisle, ran as if pursued by the devil himself, ran headlong into an immovable barrier that blocked her progress. Dazed by the impact, she began pounding on this new obstacle that stood between her and safety. A wall of some kind. For her, it meant a dead end. Overcome by hopelessness, she drew a dizzying mixture of stinging smoke, noxious fumes, and air into her lungs as she opened her mouth to scream out her frustration.

"Slow down." The deep, soothing voice came out of the darkness, freezing the scream in her throat. "Be careful, now," he said with a calm authority that broke through the utter terror that had possessed her. "Don't be scared. You'll get out in plenty of time if you do what I tell you.''

"Where are you?" Her voice came out a hoarse croak.

"Nearby. Don't worry. Just do what I say. Can you see anything?"

"No. Smoke . . ."

"Okay. Put your right hand on the wall you ran into and turn so it's on your right. Then don't move until I tell you to. Understand?"

"Yes." She did as told.

"There's a big hole in front of you. Get ready to step over it. Careful. Don't jump. Just one big step."

Cautiously, she felt with her toe for the edge of the hole. When she located it, she lengthened her stride and stepped into the blackness on the other side. "Okay."

"Good. Now put your hand on the wall like you did before. Follow it until you come to an opening. Go through it. Turn left. You'll find the way out from there."

"Aren't you coming?"

"No," he said gently. "I'm wedged in pretty tight. Go on, now. You'll be all right, and you can't help me. Get out!"

Restored to some semblance of rationality by his quiet confidence, she prepared to do as he instructed but stopped as memory returned, flooding her mind with uncertainty.

"My God! Karen." She tried to shout, but her smoke-irritated throat prevented it. "My sister."

"She left ahead of you," he said quickly. "Karen's waiting for you outside."

Having already entrusted him with her life, she had no reason now to doubt his word. She turned to make her way out of what was left of the plane. "I'll send help."

She followed his directions precisely, and after

spending a lifetime in hell in only a few seconds, she saw light. Not the blinding white light of a near-death experience. A miracle nonetheless. Red-and-blue flashing lights. Emergency lights.

She'd made it.

ONE

Rae took a sip from her cup of punch and struggled to suppress a grimace. Too sweet! Setting aside the syrupy liquid, she looked around the room. A strange gathering—from infants to the elderly, three-piece suits to jeans, the conventional to the outrageous. Ordinarily, such a diverse group of people would never have assembled in the same place at the same time, but those attending this reunion had been drawn by the extraordinary—a plane crash. *The* plane crash. Many had survived the nightmare; some had lost loved ones in it; a few, like her, had endured both.

She'd skipped the first survivors' meeting. The experience had still been too fresh in her mind. Now, however, after two years, she'd managed to come to terms with the tragedy. Almost. The fear had subsided except for an occasional nightmare, and though she still suffered pangs of guilt and flashes of anger, they were becoming less and less frequent. Only the loss persisted. It went beyond losing her sense of security, beyond, even, losing her sister. She couldn't escape the feeling that she'd left a part of herself on that broken, burning plane—some part so vague that she had yet to put a name to it, but so crucial that, without it, she would never again feel whole.

In the immediate aftermath of the tragedy, she'd set aside the sense of loss while she concentrated on getting herself and those who depended on her through the ordeal, but as her life normalized, the need to find the missing pieces reasserted itself. At first, she tried to ignore it, believing that everything would fall into place as healing progressed. It didn't. The urge to look for what would fill the nagging emptiness grew stronger with time instead of diminishing. Inevitably, it led to the survivors' reunion. Where better to look for something lost than among the people who were present when it went missing? The idea seemed logical. Unfortunately, logic wouldn't help her solve her dilemma. What she sought wouldn't be found here.

Again she surveyed the room. The reunion was supposed to provide the members of this very exclusive club with a means of exorcising the fear, anger, pain, and guilt that had resulted from their shared experience. For most, it appeared to be working, but not for her. An introvert since childhood, Rae had never been inclined to bare her soul in the presence of strangers, and that wasn't likely to change in the next few minutes.

She looked around for the exit. No point in staying any longer. No one would miss her if she left, and she had nothing to give, nothing to gain by remaining. Locating the door through which she'd entered, she stepped into the hall and paused to orient herself. Identical doors lined the long hotel corridor, and while most of them probably entered into meeting rooms similar to the one she'd just left, one concealed the elevators. Which one was anybody's guess.

"If you're looking for the way out, go right and take the second door to the left."

The rich, warm voice washed over her seemingly from out of nowhere. For a moment she once again stood amid the burning wreckage of the airplane, prepared to follow that voice to safety as she had the first time she'd heard it. Then, recovering quickly from the unwelcome flashback, she returned to reality. Trembling, she took a deep breath in an attempt to regain her composure. Two years of hearing that disembodied voice in her memory and in her dreams had given it an illusional quality—like some strange phenomenon that had emerged once for her protection and then vanished. This unexpected reminder that it did indeed belong to a real live being unsettled her.

"Sorry if I scared you," he said in the same soothing tone she knew so well. "I thought you were looking for the elevators, that's all."

Slowly, with a strange sense of reluctance, she turned toward the man who possessed the voice she knew almost intimately but whose face she'd never seen. Daniel MacKay, forty-six, veteran airline pilot. She knew the statistics. She'd read every word that had been printed about him after the accident—the praise, the accusations, and, ultimately, the vindication. In a way, she felt she knew him better than she'd ever known any man, and yet he'd never seemed quite real.

Allowing herself a few extra seconds to quiet her jittery nerves, she directed her gaze downward, lingering for a moment on the toes of his highly polished boots before letting her eyes drift upward. Slender, yet well built—she would have guessed him to be at least ten years younger than the news reports had stated—and taller than she'd imagined. At five feet eight inches, she seldom had to look very far up at anyone. This time, if she wanted to see anything above his chest, she had no choice.

Tilting her head back, she finally looked into his face to study his features as she tried to match them to the voice. It all fit, from the dark wavy hair touched with gray to the warm, friendly smile to the laugh lines that crinkled at the corners of the smoky gray eyes that engaged hers in a curious interchange. Yes, this man could calmly direct a stranger to safety while lying trapped in the wreckage of a burning aircraft, and noting the confidence in his bearing, the assurance behind his smiling eyes, Rae finally understood why she had followed his directions unquestioningly. As she continued her mute inspection, however, the friendly twinkle faded from his eyes, along with his smile.

"Sorry I bothered you," he said, his voice taking on an aloof quality that created an awkward distance between them. "Excuse me." Without waiting for a reply, he strode off toward the elevators.

Rae gazed after him. For two years she'd wondered about the man who had saved her life. What kind of person used what might have been his last seconds to help someone else? If she couldn't overcome the shock that robbed her of her ability to speak, she would never have the answers she needed.

"Wait, please," she called out, finding her voice at last.

He stopped, turning toward her with an unspoken question in his eyes.

"I didn't mean to be rude," she continued, feeling herself color as she approached him. "It's just that, well, you startled me." Her voice dwindled off as she caught up with him.

"No problem. I seem to be having that effect on a lot of people today." With a gentle half smile, he dispelled the uneasiness between them as he took the opportunity to study her features as she had his only moments before.

Unused to such scrutiny, she fidgeted under his gaze, and for the first time in her life, she envied her sister's beauty. Karen had been the striking one with her brilliant red hair, golden eyes, and a bright, friendly personality that immediately captivated people. Rae couldn't be more different. Brown hair, brown eyes—plain vanilla.

Averting her eyes to avoid seeing his reaction, she said, "You're Daniel MacKay."

"Guilty."

Surprised at his self-mocking tone, she looked back in time to see the shrug that accompanied it.

"Or so they say."

"They're wrong," she said, making no attempt to disguise the conviction she felt.

"You sound pretty sure about that."

"It was mechanical failure. Cross-wiring of the emergency systems, the investigators said. Considering the news coverage it got, everybody should know that by now."

"Not everyone understands it." He half smiled. "But you're not just anyone, are you, Iraina Garrett?"

"How did . . . oh." Following his gaze to the name tag on her shoulder, she took it off and dropped it into her purse. "I forgot I had it on."

"I'm not wearing one, so you must have recognized me from newspaper photos."

"I never saw any, not of you. And I looked for them."

"Did you?"

Realizing that she'd revealed far more than she had intended to, she changed the subject. "I was on my way downstairs."

"Mind if come with you?"

"No, why would I?"

He opened the door for her and rang for an elevator. "A lot of people at that reunion would rather walk down a hundred flights of stairs than share an elevator with me."

"I guess they still need somebody to blame, and unfortunately, you're an easy target. But that must make it twice as hard for you."

The elevator doors opened, and she stepped inside, waiting for him to join her before pushing the button for the lobby.

"Thanks for the kind words," he said as the elevator began its descent. "And the kind thoughts. These days, I don't seem to come across kindness very often."

The sincerity that emanated from his smoky gray eyes intensified her feeling of knowing him far better than their brief acquaintance would account for, and she had to fight the urge to put her arms around him and comfort him as she would a close friend. To break the spell, she smiled and forced a light tone. "You're not going to start rambling about always relying on the kindness of strangers, are you?"

He laughed, the deep, rich sound reverberating in the small space, surrounding her with its warmth, and she couldn't help joining in.

"Not now, that's for sure," he said. The elevator came to a stop, and as they exited into the luxurious hotel lobby, he paused, turning to her with the remnants of a smile still playing at the corners of his mouth. "How about a drink? I could use something to wash down the sugar from that punch, couldn't you?"

"Thank you, no," she said abruptly, caught off guard by his invitation.

"I see." All trace of familiarity vanished from his face, and once more they were strangers. "Then if you've got your garage ticket, I'll have your car brought around."

"I don't have my car. Someone's picking me up, and he probably wouldn't think to look for me in the bar, or I'd have joined you for that drink. I'm not usually so rude. Sorry."

"Forget it." His features softened. "Would this someone you're waiting for mind if I waited with you?"

"Of course not. Why would he?"

"Because if I were in his shoes, I think I'd mind very much." He spoke with a low intimacy that set her nerves atingle and left her with a warm feeling in the pit of her stomach.

"Oh," she managed a little breathlessly. "It's . . . he's my brother-in-law. He owns an automobile dealership, and he took my car in for repairs this afternoon. He's supposed to deliver it to me here. Clever conversation isn't my strong point, but if you want to . . ."

"I want to."

"Before you make up your mind about that, you'd better let me finish. I'm going to wait outside to be sure I don't miss him, and you know what summer afternoons in Texas are like."

"I can take it if you can."

Not at all sure that she could cope with the blazing Texas sun as well as with the sparks he generated, Rae led the way to a bench in the shade of a large oak tree and sat down, making room beside her for Daniel. When he'd settled himself, stretching his legs well out in front of him and draping an arm across the back of the bench, he looked over at her, a half smile tugging at one corner of his mouth.

"Would this be the time to ask if it's Miss Garrett or Mrs.?"

Pleased by his interest, she smiled. "Depends on what you want to know. I'm not married, if that's what you mean. If you want to know what to call me, 'Rae' will do."

"Rae." He spoke her name as though testing the sound of it. "Suits you. Not as exotic as 'Iraina.' "

Her smile took on a wry twist. "If there's one thing I'm not, it's exotic."

"That's not what I meant," he said in a quiet voice as he smiled back at her. "I wondered how you came by such an unusual name, that's all."

"My mother leans toward the bizarre at times. When

she went into labor with me, she was watching a weird movie about cat-people. She liked the name but wasn't sure how to spell it, so she did her own thing. I'm just glad she wasn't watching *The Hunchback of Notre Dame*."

"Don't like the name Esmeralda?"

"It's the thought of being called Quasimodo that gives me the shivers."

He burst into laughter. "You don't ever have to worry about being mistaken for Quasimodo. While I'm asking nosy questions, though, how about this brother-in-law who's picking you up? He's your sister, Karen's, husband?"

Instantly, her laughter stopped, and tears filled her eyes as she looked away to keep him from seeing. "He was."

"Oh, no!"

The words came out in an odd-sounding whoosh, and she turned back toward him. Instead of lounging comfortably beside her as he had been, he'd drawn his legs in and sat leaning forward, his elbows propped on his knees. Pale beneath his tan, he looked like he'd been sucker-punched.

"Daniel?"

He turned his head toward her but avoided her eyes.

"You remembered about Karen," Rae said. "You knew it was me that day. You've known all along."

"From the moment you spoke. I recognized your voice."

"After all this time?"

He straightened up, finally meeting her gaze, and the depth of the pain she read in his eyes made her ache for him.

"I thought I was going to die," he said, his voice low, his words meant for her alone. "Your voice was the last one I thought I'd ever hear. I'm not likely to forget it. Not in this lifetime."

"Any more than I could forget the voice of the man who saved my life."

"That's how you knew me upstairs?"

"Partly. As soon as you spoke, I knew you were the one who told me how to get out of the plane. I guessed your identity from the pictures of the crash site and from news reports. After finding the place where I got out and seeing the reports of your rescue—Captain Daniel MacKay, the last one taken from the wreckage and the most seriously injured—I assumed it had to be you."

"Oh, yeah. I did it, all right."

The anguish in his voice matched what she saw in his eyes, and she reached out, covering his hand with hers. "Yes, you did. You used your training, your experience, your courage to save a lot of lives. I've read the transcripts from the cockpit voice recorder, and I've heard what the experts have said about your performance. By all rights we should have crashed long before we did, but you did everything you could to keep that plane in the air. And you nearly pulled it off. We went down so close to the airport that emergency equipment arrived almost before the plane came to a stop. Even after the crash, while you were trapped inside with everything all around you on fire, you still managed to save lives—mine included."

"You make me sound like some kind of hero. I'm not. I'm only a man."

"A man who did everything possible to make his aircraft fly. You don't owe anyone any apologies for what you did that day."

He looked down at the comforting hand she'd placed over his, and slowly he turned it over, taking it between both of his in a gentle caress. "You're a kind and generous lady, Rae Garrett."

"If you're not a hero, I'm certainly not a saint," she said with a catch in her voice as his lightly stroking fingers sent shivers running up her arm and throughout her body in spite of the Texas heat. "At first, I blamed you for my sister's death. I hated you for it. When that didn't work anymore, I got angry because you lied to me."

"I couldn't let you go back into that plane."

"I know. But I needed the hatred and anger to help me cope with the guilt."

"Guilty of what, being alive?"

She nodded. "I always felt responsible for Karen even though she was a couple of years older than me. She was the artistic free spirit. I'm the logical one, and I was always preaching at her to think things through instead of acting on impulse. In the end, that's exactly what she did, for all the good it did her. I panicked, and yet I'm the one still here to talk about it."

"You can't blame yourself because an emergency exit door stuck."

"Neither can you. But, considering the outcome, it seems like the ultimate irony that Karen did everything right and I did everything wrong. And I even remember thinking that the emergency doors might as well be welded shut since they weren't helping me."

He squeezed her hand comfortingly, cradling it between his, and for a long time, he didn't speak as he gazed into her eyes. Finally, he said softly, "I studied the passenger list until I knew it by heart. No Karen was on it. Or on any of the other lists." He paused for a moment before going on. "I could almost make myself believe I dreamed up the name, but then I'd remember you calling out to her. So I'd check the lists again. Hell, I couldn't even find two last names that matched and might've belonged to sisters."

"Karen's not her legal name. Family and friends used it, and she did business as Karen Garrett, but she'd have been traveling as Carolyn Blackwell."

He inhaled sharply. "Yeah. That's a name I know."

A bittersweet ache filled her, and she smiled. "When I was learning to talk, I couldn't say Carolyn. It slurred into Karen and stuck."

"I'm sorry," he said in a hoarse whisper. Pausing, he cleared his throat before continuing. "I wanted to believe your sister got out okay. Most did. And I promised you she'd be all right."

Wordlessly, Rae slipped her hand from between his. Reaching up, she gently traced the almost invisible scar that began above his right ear and ran across to the corner of his mouth, as if by the gesture she could somehow erase the one tangible sign of the pain he'd endured and, by doing so, ease the inner suffering that continued to torment him.

He accepted her touch, intrigued by its effect on him. The mere contact of her fingertips to his cheek seemed to free him of some undefined burden, and for the first time in two years, he didn't dread the future. Unable to help himself, he smiled.

"Guess I should've found a better plastic surgeon."

She jerked her hand away from his face as if she'd been burned and looked down at the ground, blurting out, "Your doctor did a beautiful job, and you know it."

"Why, thank you . . . I think."

A faint blush spread across her cheeks. "I shouldn't have done that. We hardly know each other."

"Well, it's true we just met, formally anyway, but we've been talking to each other for a couple of years now. At least we have in my head."

She looked up, turning to meet his gaze, her brown-gold eyes aglitter with absolute understanding as she gave a slight nod.

"You, too?" he asked softly. "Good. At least I wasn't the only one hearing voices. One voice. Asleep, awake . . . you were always there. And sometimes I really wished you'd give me a break and go away."

She smiled. "Me, too. But now that we've met again, maybe it'll stop."

"Now I don't want it to. I've gotten kind of used to it, and even though the words never changed, I think it helped us get to know each other in a strange sort of way. Well enough, anyway, to skip the awkward stage and go straight to the friendship part." He paused. "Unless you'd rather end it here and now."

"Friends are pretty special in my book. I'd never turn one away without a very good reason."

He smiled and relaxed, stretching his legs out in front of him again.

"So, friend," she continued, a teasing glint in her eyes, "I need a favor."

"Name it."

"Brave man. You didn't even ask what I want you to do."

"Lay it on me, but I warn you, if I jump up and start running, the answer's no."

She grinned back at him, brushing her wind-tossed honey-brown hair out of her face with both hands. "Will you stay here for a few minutes and watch for a blue-and-gray Chevy Blazer—one of the little S-Ten models with a Texas Rangers bumper sticker on the back—while I try to track down my brother-in-law? He's late, and I don't want to miss him if he shows up while I'm phoning."

"Hurry back. I'll wait right here."

Daniel watched her walk away from him into the hotel. His dream come true. Literally. She'd been with him from the moment they'd first spoken to each other, nothing more than two voices in the dark. Still, they'd connected in some basic way, and until today, he hadn't even realized it. Maybe, as peculiar as it seemed, she was responsible for keeping him from giving in to utter despair when everything had appeared hopeless.

He'd felt his life had ended when his plane crashed.

Certainly, it had changed. He would never fly again. Not for a scheduled passenger airline, and while the company accepted the conclusion of the National Transportation Safety Board that he had cut power to his one good engine because cross-wiring of the emergency systems indicated it was the one on fire, his fellow pilots weren't so easy to satisfy. He had crashed his plane, killed and injured his passengers. In their eyes, the ultimate responsibility for that lay with him, no matter what conditions might have prevailed. It was part of their training, and until he'd looked at it from the other side, he'd believed it, too. Maybe part of him still did.

Intellectually, he knew he couldn't have predicted fire in the right engine when the warning light in the cockpit showed the left one disabled. Emotionally, it wasn't so easy, especially when so many blamed him for the tragedy. When he'd read about the survivors' reunion, he'd thought it the last place on earth he wanted to be. According to the attorneys involved in litigation over the accident, it was the last place he should be. Still, he'd come. And he'd found one person who believed in him.

Rae. With those wide brown eyes that shone with sincerity and honey-colored hair that fell straight to her shoulders before curling slightly under, she more than lived up to the promise of the voice. Ah, yes, the voice—quiet, genuine. A healing voice.

"That's an interesting smile. Win the lottery while I was gone?"

He looked up, his smile broadening as he reached for her hand to draw her down beside him. "Just daydreaming."

"Dream you saw my Blazer?"

"Nope. You didn't have any luck, either?"

"He left the car lot about two and a half hours ago driving my truck. He's had plenty of time to get here."

"Worried?"

She shrugged. "With Steve, it could be anything. He might've stopped somewhere and lost track of time. I'm more concerned about finding a way home."

"Forget it. I'll be happy to give you a ride."

"Thanks, but it's quite a drive."

"Dallas or Forth Worth? It doesn't make much difference. We're about halfway between."

She laughed. "But you don't understand. I don't live in the immediate Metroplex."

"No problem. It's right on my way."

"How do you know?"

"Come on. Let's go get my car."

The valet delivered the car, and Rae settled comfortably into the passenger's seat while Daniel slid in behind the wheel.

"Nice," she commented, running a hand over the leather upholstery. "I always thought if I had a sports car, I'd want a Mercedes."

"Yeah, I like it." He put it in gear and prepared to drive off. "It's got a few years and a few miles on it, but it's beginning to develop character. Only one problem."

"Gas mileage?"

He looked over at her and grinned. "Nope. Operator problem. I don't know where we're going."

"Decatur," she said hesitantly, half expecting him to change his mind, but he didn't even seem fazed by it. "Know where it is?"

"Sure do." He guided the car onto the street. "Like I said, right on my way."

"To where?" she asked skeptically. "Oklahoma?"

"To where I'm going. There's no reason we can't make a little detour, though. Since your brother-in-law stood you up, why not have dinner with me? I know a nice little restaurant in Forth Worth. It's quiet. Food's good. Italian—like it?"

"Love it, but I . . ."

"Can't or won't?"

"Can't. My housekeeper gets off at six, and I haven't lined up a baby-sitter for the girls this evening. Since their dad left me stranded, I can't even count on him."

"Their dad's the brother-in-law you've been talking about?"

She nodded.

"Karen's children." His voice sounded subdued, and his eyes clouded over, making it difficult to tell what was going on behind them.

"My nieces live with me now. That's how Karen wanted it, and Steve didn't object."

"Fatherhood too much for him?"

Rae studied Daniel's features, trying to see behind the mask that obscured the kind, warm nature of the man she was only beginning to know. For a long time he stared straight ahead, urging the car down the highway as fast as the law allowed. Finally, he gave her a sideways glance.

"Sorry. None of my business."

"No. But I don't mind telling you about it, and anyway, you're not far off the mark. He's not really cut out to be a single parent. Besides, I love having the girls with me, and they seem happy."

He smiled, and the mask fell away, once again revealing the man underneath. "Who wouldn't be happy with you?"

"Have dinner with us instead. No dim lights or soft music, but Elena's a good cook, and there's always enough for one more. And the girls love having company. Of course, dinner with a three-year-old and a five-year-old can be loud and messy, but if you're up to it . . ."

"Wouldn't it be a question of whether or not your nieces would want me at their dinner table?"

The pieces fell into place, and the reason for his strange reaction when she had mentioned the girls became clear. Guilt. She placed her hand over his where it rested on the gearshift knob.

"They're babies. They won't make the connection between you and the accident, and even if they did, they wouldn't blame you. They're great kids."

He turned his hand over and entwined his fingers with hers. "Like their aunt."

His low, soothing tone, along with the half smile she knew she would dream about, magnified his words into the nicest compliment she'd ever received. Once again she felt herself enveloped in the warm familiarity of a friendship much deeper than could be explained by their short acquaintance. Instead of alarming her, she found it comforting, and the rest of the drive was accomplished in companionable silence. To her, the distance had never seemed shorter as she directed him to her home five blocks from the town square.

"It's the white house on the corner," she said as they neared their destination.

He slowed, following her directions to the old Victorian two-story house that had recently been restored to its original grandeur, complete with a wraparound porch that ran the entire length of two sides of the building, and a freshly painted white fence enclosing a beautifully landscaped lawn. But it was the vehicle parked beside the house that caught Daniel's attention.

"The one with the blue-and-gray Blazer in the drive?" he asked with a touch of amusement.

"That's the one." Her voice held no trace of humor. "My truck seems to have found its way home without me, doesn't it?"

TWO

Daniel pulled up in front of the house, stopping the car next to the curb. As he walked around to open the passenger door, two tiny pairs of eyes peering at him through a window over the porch caught his attention, and the moment Rae stepped from the car, two bundles of energy masquerading as little girls burst from the house and raced down the front walk to the gate.

"Auntie Rae! Auntie Rae!" they squealed impatiently as they looked out from between the slats of the gate.

Smiling at their enthusiastic greeting, she covered completely any trace of irritation she might feel at having been abandoned sixty miles from home. "Hi there," she called out to them. To Daniel, she said in a more moderate tone, "Come in," then reached for the latch and swung the gate open.

The two youngsters allowed just enough room and just enough time for him and Rae to enter the yard and close the gate behind them before once more breaking into excited chatter, the words spilling out so rapidly that he couldn't always tell which child was saying what.

"Daddy came to visit."

"Elena made a pie."

"We helped."

"Can we grow some flowers?"

"She went home."

"Did you go to a party?"

"Whoa," Rae said loudly enough to temporarily slow down the barrage. "Don't I get a hug first?"

She knelt on the sidewalk and drew both children into a tight embrace, apparently oblivious to the bright red, sticky-looking stain on the front of the younger girl's playsuit.

Daniel smiled down at the three of them. "Do you always receive such a great greeting?"

"Most of the time," Rae answered, her voice muffled by her nieces' energetic hugs.

Unsmiling, the older girl gazed up at him with a mature expression that far outstripped her five years. For a moment, he had the uncanny feeling that he was seeing Rae as a child. They had the same large brown-gold eyes, and though her niece's chin-length hair was several shades lighter than Rae's, it fell straight from the part on one side and curled under at the ends. "Sometimes we don't know when Auntie Rae is coming home," she said to Daniel. Turning her attention back to Rae, she frowned. "You're late."

"I'm sorry." Rae responded to the admonishment with sincerity, conveying her concern with her manner as well as her words. "I put my car in the shop today, and I didn't have a way to get home until this gentleman offered me a ride. Daniel," she said, smiling up at him, "I'd like you to meet my nieces." She put an arm around the solemn blond child and gave her a squeeze. "This is Kristen. The little red-haired bundle of raw energy is Erin. Girls, say hello to Daniel."

Kristen stepped forward and extended her hand. "How do you do, Mr. Daniel."

He quickly suppressed his surprise at such a formal greeting as he bent down to take her little hand in his, giving it a gentle shake. "Hello, Kristen. It's very nice to meet you."

"Me, too," Erin shouted with none of her sister's self-control. Her halo of red curls bouncing, she jumped up and down, holding her arms up to him. "Carry me, Dan-yul."

Grinning, he reached down and lifted her into his arms. "At your service, your Highness."

A frown puckered Kristen's face as she shook her head. "She's awful spoiled, Mr. Daniel."

Laughing, Rae got to her feet, brushing the dust from the knees of her cream-colored slacks. "Yes, she is. And judging from this," she said, pointing to the red smear that had transferred itself onto her blouse, "Elena's already given you your dinner."

"Elena went home," Kristen replied impatiently. "I told you 'while ago. Daddy ate with us."

"And it was delicious." A man of medium height whom Daniel guessed to be in his mid-thirties came out onto the porch. Showing off his perfectly even teeth with a salesman's smile, he walked to the top of the steps and stopped as if posing. Immaculately groomed, with not so much as one blond hair out of place, and dressed in what could only be described as deliberate casual, he appeared the type who never drifted more than ten paces away from a mirror.

"Hello, Steve," Rae said evenly, though sparks flew from her eyes. "I didn't expect you to be here."

"Brought your truck." Again he flashed a smile that encompassed both Rae and Daniel.

"You were supposed to pick me up, remember? If you had, you could have saved yourself this trip."

"That's okay. I didn't mind."

Rae marched up the steps to confront him eye to eye. "And how did you think I would get home?"

"Don't blow a gasket, Rae. I can explain." With his Cheshire-cat grin still in place, he took a couple of steps backward, lifting his hands in mock surrender, a gesture that seemed calculated to show off his gold Rolex watch. "I forgot all about you until I was already halfway here. I figured by the time I drove all the way back, you'd have scrounged up a ride. And you did." He reached around Rae to hold out a perfectly manicured hand to Daniel. "Steve Blackwell. These are my pretty little girls."

Daniel shook the offered hand, but before he could say anything, Erin interrupted. Lurching toward Steve with her arms outstretched, she demanded, "Take me, Daddy."

Steve backed away, reaching out to tousle her red curls. "Not a chance, carrot-top. Not until your aunt Rae gets you cleaned up." Ignoring the pouting child as she laid her head on Daniel's shoulder and slipped her arms around his neck, Steve continued as if the interruption hadn't taken place. "Didn't catch your name."

"Daniel MacKay."

Steve's eyes narrowed into angry ice-blue slits as he glared at Daniel. "Daniel MacKay," he repeated, spitting out the words as if they tasted bad. "You're the b—"

"Stop right there, Steve." Rae placed a hand on his chest and backed him up a few more steps.

"But—" he sputtered.

"Not another word," she ordered. As she turned to Kristen, her voice softened. "Kris, will you take Erin upstairs and see if you can find her a clean playsuit before she gets red spots on us all?"

The girl nodded.

"Thanks," Rae said gently. "I'll be up in a few minutes to get Eri washed and changed. Okay?"

Daniel lowered Erin to the porch, and the two girls disappeared into the house.

"Perhaps I'd better go," Daniel said quietly.

"Damn right," Steve began, but again Rae cut him off.

"No." Her sharply spoken reply sounded like a command. Pausing, she took a deep breath, and in a tone that reflected her restored composure, she continued, speaking to Daniel. "Please don't leave. I invited you to dinner, and I hope you'll stay."

"What's going on, Rae?" her brother-in-law demanded. "He killed Karen, and I want him out of this house right now."

"This is *my* house, in case you've forgotten." Refusing to be intimidated, she stood her ground. "And Daniel is my guest. If you can't be civil, then *you* leave."

"Since when do you give the red-carpet treatment to murderers?" Steve shot back.

In an unconsciously protective gesture, she stepped back to stand beside Daniel as she placed a comforting hand on his arm. Though she glared at her brother-in-law, her voice remained deadly quiet. "I've had quite enough of you for one day, Steve. You left me stranded sixty miles from home, you ate my dinner, and now you're trying to tell me who I can invite into my home. Well, forget it. *You* are the one who's going to leave. The sooner, the better."

"Can't. I drove your truck out here, remember?" he said sullenly, resembling a pouting child. "I'm waiting for somebody to pick me up."

"Then you can wait out in the heat like I waited two hours for you." She opened the door and motioned for Daniel to enter before she followed him inside. Closing the door behind her, she leaned back against it as she gazed apologetically at him. "I'm sorry."

"It's nothing I haven't heard before."

"That doesn't make it right," she said, her voice

full of distress. "I had no idea Steve would be here, or I'd never have let you walk into it unprepared. I really am sorry."

Placing his hands on her shoulders, he forced her to look up to meet his eyes. "It's not your fault. Hell, you can't even blame your brother-in-law for the way he feels. His whole life changed because of something I did."

She opened her mouth to speak, but he stopped her by touching a finger to her lips.

"Right or wrong," he continued, "that's how he and a lot of others see it. And the fact is, I did take action that brought that plane down. Who can say whether or not it was justified?"

She looked down, resting her forehead against his chest. "The NTSB. They cleared you."

Her words washed over him like some magical healing balm that seeped into every pore and made him feel alive again. He wanted to take her in his arms, to hold her close and enjoy the strange restorative effect she had on him, but he fought the impulse, settling instead for her nearness, the touch of her face on his chest, the soft, warm feel of her shoulders under his hands, and her sweet, heady scent. That would do until . . .

"Auntie Rae." Kristen's voice dragged him back to reality, and both he and Rae turned toward it. Hand in hand, the two little girls stood at the bottom of the stairway. "We changed Erin's clothes."

"So I see." Rae walked over and gave each of her nieces a hug as she sat down on the stairs to examine the result of their efforts. "Good job. And you did it all by yourselves."

Kristen's eyes brightened at the praise, and she smiled the first smile Daniel had seen from her. He had a hunch Kristen didn't waste her smiles, and of those she gave, he'd bet most were reserved for her aunt. Little wonder. Rae had a way of emphasizing the things that made a person want to smile and ignoring the things that might bring on a frown or even tears—like the extra button at the top of Erin's playsuit and the extra buttonhole at the bottom. She didn't even mention them.

"I washed her hands and face," Kristen said shyly.

"I helped," Erin chimed in, bobbing up and down in a continuing display of perpetual motion.

Rae laughed. "Your daddy's outside waiting for someone to pick him up. Why don't you keep him company while I put together some dinner for Daniel and me?"

"Cookie's probably coming to get him," Kristen muttered, frowning as she took Erin's hand. "Come on."

"No." Erin pulled out of her sister's grasp and ran to Daniel. Wrapping both arms around his legs, she said, "Hold me, Dan-yul."

Before he could pick her up, though, Rae reached over and disengaged the child's hold on him. "Not this time, little one. We've already passed that sticky red stuff around quite enough," she said, indicating the matching spots that had been left on his shirt and her blouse. "Smells like strawberry."

"Strawberry pie," Erin shouted with glee. "I helped."

Getting up from the stairs, Rae gave the girl a pat on the bottom. "Now that you're all clean and shiny, I'm going to see about getting this mess off Daniel and me." She looked at him. "I hadn't counted on someone eating our dinner. How do you feel about potluck?"

"Sounds great, but don't go to any trouble."

She smiled. "You went out of your way for me. Besides, I have to eat anyway, and it's as easy to cook for two as it is for one. Dinner'll be a while, though."

"I'm not punching a time clock."

"Let's go out to the kitchen, then." With Rae lead-ing the way, they started off toward the back of the house.

"Come on, Erin." Kristen's dejected-sounding mumble carried barely far enough for them to hear. "We have to go outside."

Rae stopped dead in her tracks and turned around, looking past Daniel at the girls. "Kris, you don't have to go out if you don't want to. I thought you might want to spend some time with Steve, that's all. If you don't, come to the kitchen with us."

"Do you mind?" Kristen asked hesitantly.

Rae glanced at Daniel.

He grinned. "Not at all. Where else could I have three lovely ladies like you all to myself?"

"Okeydokey," Erin yelled, running ahead of them while Kristen followed at a more dignified pace.

Rae smiled at him. "Be careful what you ask for; you may get it with a vengeance."

By the time they got to the kitchen, the children had already seated themselves at the table, Erin in her own booster seat and Kristen on a thick book that looked like a volume from an encyclopedia.

"First, the strawberry pie." Rae dampened some paper towels, and with the girls watching intently, she and Daniel went to work on the spots Erin had bestowed on each of them.

After a few minutes, Daniel looked up. "That's about as good as it's going to get."

Examining the pink circle on his formerly white shirt, Rae sighed. "You're paying dearly for your good deed. Maybe I can make it up to you with dinner." She opened the refrigerator and, after a brief examination of its contents, said, "I've got salad stuff and not much else. Wouldn't you know it, tomorrow's Elena's shopping day."

"Fortunately, I love salad, and I'm a whiz at chopping and slicing."

She gave him a wry smile. "You're a good sport, but I'd counted on something a little more substantial." She turned back to the refrigerator as if making certain she hadn't overlooked anything.

Quietly, Kristen slipped out of her chair and went over to stand beside Rae. "Auntie Rae," she said in a child's whisper that could be clearly heard by anyone who happened to be in the room.

Absently, Rae dropped an arm across Kristen's shoulders. "What is it, sweetie?"

"Emergency spaghetti."

"Good thinking, Kris." Rae scooped the little girl into her arms and gave her a kiss before setting her back on her feet. "Perfect. Emergency spaghetti." She turned to Daniel. "You did say you like Italian?"

"Sure." He paused before asking hesitantly, "What exactly is emergency spaghetti?"

Rae burst out laughing. "When we have spaghetti, we make a double batch of sauce and freeze half for emergencies—like tonight."

He grinned. "What can I do to help?"

"Looks like you already have your hands full. And your lap, too," Rae said, noting that without bothering to ask, Erin had planted herself on Daniel's knees. "She likes being the center of attention, but you don't have to pick her up every time she demands it."

"I'm enjoying this. Take it from an expert, quiet dinners at home alone aren't what they're cracked up to be. Company's nice for a change."

"You've eaten alone often enough to qualify as an expert?" she asked with the lift of an eyebrow.

His grin broadened. "Well, nearly."

"Uh-huh," she said skeptically as she put the spaghetti pot on to boil. Without so much as the briefest pause, she turned her attention to the salad. "Dinner won't be long now. The sauce only needs heating."

"In the microwave," Kristen informed him after climbing back into her chair.

While Rae completed the dinner preparations, he chatted with the two little girls and quickly discovered that keeping up with them required considerable mental agility as they leapt from subject to subject, exhibiting vivid imaginations. Unprepared for the variety of questions they threw at him, he struggled to answer, amazed at the number of facts they expected him to have at his fingertips. They kept him so completely involved that before he knew it, Rae had dinner ready.

Instead of moving everyone into the dining room, she served the meal at the kitchen table. That suited him. He knew of no five-star restaurant anywhere that could match the ambience of the cozy little kitchen. And dinner was delicious.

"Best emergency spaghetti I ever tasted," he said, downing the last bite.

Rae laughed. "It's the *only* emergency spaghetti you've ever had."

He laughed, too, and with Kristen's help, the two of them set about cleaning up the kitchen. By the time they finished, Erin had fallen asleep in her chair.

"That's Erin's subtle way of letting me know it's time I got her to bed," Rae said, picking up the sleeping child. "It's way past your bedtime, too, Kris."

"I'm not sleepy, Auntie Rae." She opened her eyes extra wide as if to prove it.

"Okay, a few more minutes. Why don't you show Daniel to the living room while I take Erin upstairs." To Daniel, Rae said, "How about coffee and a piece of that strawberry pie when I get back?"

"Just coffee for me." He patted his stomach. "I'd have gone easy on the emergency spaghetti if I'd known you had strawberry pie left."

With a laugh, Rae disappeared through a door he guessed led to the back stairs.

"The living room is this way, Mr. Daniel," Kristen said in a mature manner that many adults he knew hadn't yet mastered.

"Lead on, Kristen." He followed the little girl into the hall. "And call me Daniel. Forget about the Mr. part."

"It's not polite to call grown-ups just by their first name."

"That's a good idea most of the time." Leave it to a five-year-old to make him feel like a disobedient child. "Sometimes it's okay, though, and I wouldn't mind if you called me Daniel. Erin does."

She let out a long-suffering sigh. "Erin is impossible."

He smiled, barely managing to suppress a laugh. "She's on the high-spirited side, but don't be too tough on her."

Kristen stopped in front of a large, heavy door and pushed it open. "In here, Mr. Daniel. Please, have a seat."

He followed her into the room. Like the exterior, the inside of the house had been either amazingly well cared for over the years or meticulously restored. Yet it retained a feeling of being lived in, a sense of home, unlike so many houses that had been renovated and then kept picture-perfect until they acquired a museumlike atmosphere. Two kids probably helped. And Rae. She had a talent for seeing into a person's soul and using what she found there to make him comfortable.

Kristen seated herself on the sofa facing the fireplace. As he started to sit down, however, a portrait of a breathtakingly beautiful woman caught his attention. Hanging over the mantel, it dominated the room, and, fascinated, he walked over to examine it more closely. Auburn hair a shade darker than Erin's framed the face, displaying flawless alabaster skin to perfection as it ac- centuated the gold sparkle of eyes that some would call hazel for lack of a more accurate description. Karen. The woman couldn't be anyone else.

"That's my mother," Kristen said as if to confirm his conjecture. She left her place on the sofa and came over to stand beside him.

He looked down at the little girl, who craned her neck to get a glimpse of the portrait, and without thinking, he bent down to pick her up. She didn't object, though, as he brought her closer to eye level with the portrait, which she studied as intently as he did.

"She's beautiful," he said after a while, unable to gauge the child's reaction.

Unsmiling, she continued to gaze at the picture. "Everybody says that."

"Erin looks a lot like her."

"Everybody says that, too." Neither her voice nor her expression changed, but he felt a subtle withdrawal. "She died."

"I know." He looked back at the portrait. Whatever was going on behind Kristen's serious little face, he couldn't begin to guess. Finally he said, "She's beautiful in a different way from Rae, don't you think?"

Kristen brightened almost imperceptibly. "Oh, yes."

"Nobody could miss your mother's kind of beauty. It sort of reaches out and grabs you and makes you take notice. Rae's kind is quieter, softer."

"The hugging kind," the little girl agreed.

"That's it." He liked Kristen's choice of words. They described Rae exactly. "And I think anybody who happened to resemble Rae would be very lucky."

Kristen's eyes lit up as though someone had turned on a lamp behind them, and her lips twitched almost into a smile. "I think so, too. You can put me down now, please."

He lowered her to the floor, and when she once again took a seat on the sofa, he sat at the opposite end. They had barely settled themselves when Rae came through the door carrying a silver tray that held the coffee.

"Find something to talk about while I was gone?" she asked as she set the tray on the coffee table.

Kristen answered for both Daniel and herself. "My mother's picture."

Rae glanced up at the picture, then at Daniel, before turning her attention to pouring coffee. "We had those done from the photographic portraits we made to hang at the studio."

"Those?" he asked. "You have more than one?"

"One of me." Rae gazed up at her sister's portrait. "Nothing as stunning as that."

"I'd like to judge that for myself. Is the other one around here someplace?"

"Upstairs. Two objects that size in the same room would be one too many, so mine's in my bedroom." She shrugged. "It was either there or the attic."

"At least the attic didn't get it," he said, pausing to stir cream into his coffee and take a sip from his cup. The rich-tasting liquid gave him a warm, comfortable feeling—something he was beginning to get used to. "Where would I go to see the original photographs?"

Rae slipped her shoes off and settled into the soft sofa cushions as she drew Kristen into an easy embrace. "Seems like a lot of trouble to me, but the photos hang in the lobby of Garrett and Garrett Studios at Hulen Mall in Forth Worth and at the Riverwalk in New Orleans."

"Garrett and Garrett," he repeated thoughtfully. "I know where that is. I've passed by it at Hulen Mall. You're a photographer?"

"We do glamour shots. A client comes in; we do a complete make-over—makeup, hair, even clothing on occasion. Then we photograph our subject at his or her best."

"Queen for a day."

"More like star for a day."

"Interesting concept."

"It was Karen's idea. She did some modeling as a teenager and learned a lot about what goes on behind the camera as well. She thought everyone ought to have the opportunity to look and feel glamorous at least once. I agreed. So we pooled our money and our talents and opened Garrett and Garrett Studios."

"What kind of clients do you get? Housewives, mothers, working women?"

"All of the above plus jocks, professional people, and high school students, both female and male. We do a lot of portraits for people to use as gifts, and occasionally we get an aspiring actor or model who's putting together a portfolio. Most, though, are average, everyday people who want to look and feel like a movie star for a little while, and they want the experience captured on film."

"And you used yourselves as examples," he said, nodding toward Karen's portrait.

"That was Karen's idea, too. Of course, no amount of makeup and glitter will ever make me look glamorous, but she insisted."

"She must have been smart as well as beautiful to have realized how side-by-side portraits of the two of you would look. The perfect contrast—smart sophistication and quiet elegance."

Rae laughed. "Nobody was better than Karen at bringing out a person's best features, and she did her best with me, but don't imagine for a second that anyone even notices my picture hanging beside hers. Karen's photo dazzles. Mine never could."

Kristen interrupted. "But Auntie Rae's picture is quiet, Mr. Daniel. It's reeeal quiet."

"Bet it is." He winked his understanding at the little girl.

"Quiet?" Rae looked over Kristen's head at him. "What's that supposed to mean?"

"Oh . . . nothing," Kristen replied with exaggerated innocence.

"Nothing, indeed." But Rae didn't press further for an explanation as she smoothed back her niece's hair and gave her a kiss on the cheek. "You've stayed up long enough. Go on upstairs and change into your nightie. I'll be up in a few minutes to tuck you in."

"Yes, ma'am." Like a miniature adult, Kristen slipped off the sofa. Extending her hand, she approached Daniel. "I'm glad you came to visit us, Mr. Daniel. Will you come back sometime?"

He took her little hand between his and gave it a friendly squeeze. "I'd like to very much, Kristen. Thanks to you and Erin and Rae, this evening's been a real treat for me."

Again she didn't quite smile, though her eyes danced. "Do you like picnics, Mr. Daniel?"

He chuckled. "To tell the truth, it's been so long since my last picnic that I barely remember it, but it sounds like fun."

"No more stalling, Kris," Rae said.

"I'm being polite, like you taught me." Indignation tinged the child's voice, and with a sideways glance at Daniel, she went on. "Now that I'm a big girl, you don't have to tuck me in if you're too busy."

"Have I ever been too busy to say good night to you?"

"Nope." Kristen skipped out of the room and disappeared up the stairs.

Daniel watched her go. "I look at her and see a child. She speaks, and I hear a little girl's voice, but the words and the disposition are so . . . mature."

"It worries me sometimes." Rae shrugged and sighed. "Other times, she's like any other child, laughing, running, playing. She's shy, though. It takes her a long time to accept someone new.''

"I noticed."

"But you charmed both the girls. It amazed me how quickly Kris warmed to you.''

"Chilly kind of warmth."

"For Kris meeting someone new, it's a regular heat wave. You nearly got her to smile. And she invited you to our picnic on Saturday.''

"Invited me? Did I miss something?" He shifted his position and, with one hand, reached around to try to alleviate the dull, aching throb that had started again in the small of his back.

"Kris'd never ask you herself. That's her way of getting me to do it for her. She doesn't realize you've probably made plans for the weekend already.''

"I haven't. But I don't want to horn in on a family outing, and I couldn't help noticing it wasn't your idea to invite me.''

"Kris beat me to it. We're planning to leave here about ten-thirty and drive up to Black Creek Lake. You'd be more than welcome.''

"What do you want me to bring?"

"A big appetite and lots of patience." She put her empty cup on the tray. "I'd better get Kris settled for the night. Excuse me for a few minutes.''

Rae walked slowly up the stairs, disappearing around the same bend that had taken Kristen from his sight. Alone, Daniel finished his coffee. Setting the cup aside, he leaned back to rest his head on the sofa as, with his eyes closed, he tried to will away the pain. Damn. Why now? Why did it have to intrude on the nicest evening he'd enjoyed in years? Well, he wouldn't let it spoil everything. He'd grit his teeth and take it.

Rae's hand on his shoulder caught him by surprise. He hadn't heard her come back into the room, and, startled, he opened his eyes to discover her standing behind him looking down into his face. Even upside down, she looked lovely.

"Lean forward," she said softly, prodding him gently on the shoulder.

He smiled, a little embarrassed at being caught indulging in self-pity. "Forget it. I'm all right."

"Your back hurts. Maybe I can help." She gripped his shoulders firmly and urged him forward. He gave in. Arguing wouldn't be worth the effort. Obediently, he sat up and propped his elbows on his knees.

Alternately kneading and rubbing, she started at his shoulders, her amateur but competent ministrations easing the tension out of his neck and upper back, and he began to relax. He closed his eyes to better enjoy the soothing massage that threatened to put him to sleep until she began to slowly slide her hands down his back. Even through his shirt, the feel of her hands gliding over his body created in him a subtle and not-unwelcome tension of their own.

"Stop me when I get to where it hurts," she murmured, leaning over the back of the sofa so that her hands could continue their journey downward.

Stop her? Not likely. Her hands, stroking and rubbing their way down his back, along with her utterly feminine scent, produced the most incredible anesthetic he'd ever encountered. It might not make his back stop hurting, but it would certainly keep his mind off it.

THREE

Rae moved her hands slowly over Daniel's well-muscled back, her fingers automatically identifying knots of tension that required special attention, and as she methodically massaged away his discomfort, she felt him begin to relax. Gradually, she worked her way down to the spot above his belt that seemed to be causing the most distress.

"Ahhh."

His half groan, half sigh stopped her cold.

"Did I hurt you?"

"Uh-uh. Feels good."

Gingerly, she resumed the massage. When he didn't complain, she continued with more assurance until the rubdown began to affect her in a completely unexpected way. Leaning over him, she couldn't escape his uncompromisingly masculine scent, and the friction of her hands moving over his body seemed to generate heat in spite of the insulation provided by his shirt. It didn't make sense. Why should a simple back rub take on this feeling of intimacy?

Disturbed by her strange reaction, she ended the massage and walked around to claim her seat on the sofa.

With a sigh, Daniel leaned back against the cushions. "Better?" she asked, stalling while her pulse slowed to its normal rhythm.

He smiled, all trace of pain-induced strain gone from his face. "You're a miracle worker. When it starts, nothing helps. Not usually, that is."

"Happen often?"

"Often enough."

"Can't you get help for it?"

"Sure. They all prescribe the standard treatment—exercises and pills. I've gotten used to the physical therapy, but I prefer to do without the painkillers."

Annoyed by the archaic attitude that prevented him from using all available methods to relieve his pain, she mumbled, "Macho nonsense."

His deep, gentle laugh filled the room as he reached over to take her hand in his. "Not entirely. Those drugs are powerful. If I take them, I can't drive or operate machinery or do anything else that could be affected by a slowed reaction time. I'd be stuck in my apartment for the most part, and I don't want to spend the rest of my life looking at four walls and a ceiling, even if it means my back'll hurt sometimes."

Embarrassed, she looked down at his hand holding hers. "That was stupid."

"It was concern, not stupidity."

His soothing voice enveloped her in its warmth and compelled her to raise her eyes to meet his smoky gray ones.

"I didn't stop to think that the medication might be worse than the injury."

"As long as I can keep it in perspective, it doesn't bother me . . . much." He gave a short, humorless laugh. "Keeps me off the flight deck, and frankly, that suits New World Airways just fine. If I'd come out of it fit, they'd have had to find some other reason to ground me."

"Would you want to fly again?"

"Yeah." His dark eyes broke away from hers as he looked past her and retreated to some distant, private place. His mood change lasted no more than a moment before, with a rueful half smile and a shrug of resignation, he rejoined her in the present. "Yeah. But that's not going to happen."

"Even if your back gets better?"

"Not a chance. Be bad for business. Who'd get on a plane knowing I was up front? Imagine what would happen to reservations if the public found out I was flying again. Hell, I'm lucky New World didn't pension me off like they did my copilot."

"I forgot you still worked for them."

"Forgot?" His eyes widened, and a curious expression crossed his face. "Is there anything about me you don't know?"

"I . . . it was in the newspapers," she said, unsettled by the hint of annoyance in his tone. "After the NTSB released its findings, the airline announced you'd be working at the flight academy. But the article didn't include your title."

"Instructor. I teach other pilots not to do what I did."

"As long as you feel like that, you shouldn't be flying."

He looked stunned. Recovering quickly, however, he broke into a grin. "Touché. Sorry about the sarcasm. I'm usually better at keeping it under control."

"I didn't mean it like that," she said, mentally kicking herself for her abrupt remark. "But as long as you blame yourself—"

He stopped her by touching a finger to her lips. "I know. You're right. I need to let it go, and I've been working on it. The reunion set me back some. Going there probably wasn't the healthiest decision I could have made. Somehow, though, I can't bring myself to regret it.''

His eyes mirrored the sincerity in his voice, momentarily robbing her of the ability to speak. Swallowing hard, she forced herself not to look away while she collected her thoughts.

"You might when you hear what I'm about to tell you," she finally managed. Losing her courage, she looked down at her hands. "Steve filed suit over Karen's death. Among other things, he accuses you of incompetence.''

"I know." He gave her hand a comforting squeeze. "I recognized the name Carolyn Blackwell the minute you said it—both from the casualty list and from papers related to the suit.''

"You've been served already?''

"Sure. When it was filed.''

A strange mixture of relief and annoyance flooded through her. "Why didn't you say something?''

"Like what? Go after the manufacturer, the airline, the maintenance crew, but leave me out of it? It doesn't work that way, Rae. Nine lawsuits are still pending. I'm named in every single one of them.''

"But I don't have to testify at all nine of them—only Steve's.''

"And that bothers you?''

"It doesn't bother you?''

"Of course. The idea of sitting in a courtroom being raked over the coals in front of the whole world doesn't exactly thrill me, and knowing you'll be there makes it that much worse. The only way I'm going to get through it, though, is to take each day as it comes, and today, I'm enjoying your company. I'll deal with the trials one at a time.''

"If not for you, I wouldn't even be around to give testimony.''

"Don't do that to yourself. You didn't ask for this.

None of us did, and who knows? Steve might settle his suit before it ever gets to court."

"Not likely. New World made him a generous offer, and he rejected it."

"Well, then you'll have no choice. Whatever happens, I won't blame you for what you say on the witness stand."

"Except for telling how the girls have been affected, there's not a lot I can say. The technical stuff—that's somebody else's headache."

"Yeah." He sighed deeply and covered his face with both hands for a moment. When he once again turned to face her, he looked tired. "I've enjoyed today more than anything in a long time. Being with you feels good. I'd hate for something like a lawsuit to ruin my chances of spending other evenings with you. We share some pretty disturbing memories, though, and if you don't want me around, tell me straight out. I'll understand."

"I thought you should know, that's all."

"Thanks, but I think I can handle it. Can you?"

She nodded. "Maybe after the trial, we'll finally be able to put it behind us and get on with our lives."

Without answering, he looked away, retreating to his private sanctuary.

Where were her brains? What gross insensitivity to speak of putting the tragedy behind her to a man who didn't have that luxury—wouldn't have for years, if ever. Nine lawsuits. She could barely cope with the prospect of one.

The weariness etched in the lines of his face betrayed his internal turmoil, and for the first time, she fully understood the depth of his anguish. Usually he covered it well—so well that she'd completely misread him. What she had interpreted earlier as self-pity was in truth a pain so deep that it far outstripped the survivor's guilt she'd struggled through, and so intense he could scarcely acknowledge it. Coming to terms with it would be a separate hell. No one knew better than she what it took to reduce the trauma inflicted by the plane crash to a manageable level, and he hadn't yet begun to heal.

Moving closer to him, she touched his shoulder lightly, and he reached out to draw her into his arms. For a moment she resisted, afraid that he'd misunderstood her intentions, but as he held her close and buried his face in her shoulder, she relaxed. The comfort she offered was indeed what he needed, and no one should have to confront such pain alone.

For a long time they sat sharing an embrace as intimate as any inspired by passion. Neither spoke. The intensity of their silent exchange transcended mere words. What could she say to ease his mind? What words could he speak that would lessen her loss? Still, the empathic flow of energy that had linked them from the beginning seemed to strengthen, and she could feel his pain begin to ebb.

Gradually, he loosened his arms, drawing away from her little by little until finally he placed his hands on her shoulders and leaned back to look into her eyes.

"Thanks for dinner," he said softly, with no more than a trace of huskiness left in his deep voice to betray the emotions that had so recently threatened to engulf him completely. "And thank you . . . well, just thank you. But I better go before I find myself trying to take advantage of you in a way that wouldn't make me feel very good about myself."

Unsure who would have been taking advantage of whom, she smiled.

Jamming his hands into his pants pockets, he got to his feet and drew a deep breath that he let out slowly. "Frankly, Rae, you make it much too easy for a man to forget about honor."

She laughed at his half-joking tone, glad for a break in the highly charged atmosphere, and rose from the sofa to stand beside him. "You don't make passes on the first date?"

"This isn't exactly a date," he reminded her. "And no, not at you. You're not the kind who engages in one-night stands. It'd be stupid to screw up what might turn out to be the best thing that's ever happened to me by trying to lure you into something like that."

Taken off guard by his candor, she could only stare at him.

"Come on. Walk me to the door."

Without comment, she accompanied him out onto the porch.

"Sorry if I offended you," he said when they paused at the steps.

"You didn't. It's just that people aren't usually so . . . honest."

He chuckled. "Or blunt. Anyway, it's time I left."

"It *is* getting late, and you still have to get home, wherever that is."

"Fort Worth."

"Not too bad, but Decatur wasn't on your way at all."

"Sure it was. Anywhere you wanted to go would have been on my way." He reached for her hand, cradling it between his. "Now, tell me, how's your memory?"

She smiled, studying his face for some clue to what prompted this abrupt change of subject. "Good enough, I guess."

Gently, he turned her hand over, holding it in one of his while, with his opposite index finger, he began slowly tracing figures into her open palm.

His light, teasing touch ignited sparks that traveled in a cold-hot wave up her arm and throughout her body until what had begun as a simple, playful gesture became a seductive caress that threatened her senses.

Daniel, too, appeared enthralled by the power of the

electrical charges running back and forth between them. His eyes, gazing down into hers, took on a thrilling intensity, and he drew her hand closer to him in a tantalizingly possessive manner. When he finished the number, he curled her fingers into a fist and held it completely enclosed in his hands as he murmured, "That's where you can reach me the next time you need a ride home, or any other time you want me."

"I'll remember," she whispered, struggling to control her erratic breathing and wildly thumping heart.

When he leaned closer, she instinctively lifted her face toward his. Instead of the kiss she expected, however, only his warm breath caressed her face. "Good night, Rae. Sweet dreams."

Without waiting for a response, he turned to leave, taking the steps two at a time before starting down the front walk.

Daniel MacKay. Now she had a face and a personality to go with the statistics. How misleading those lists of facts could be. Nothing she'd read had prepared her for his sense of humor, his gentleness, his strength, his vulnerability, his . . . humanness.

Leaning back against the door, she retraced the telephone number he'd etched in her palm, and the warmth his touch generated returned to ensure that her dreams would indeed be sweet.

Her daydreams as well.

The feeling of well-being left from Daniel's visit stayed with Rae through the night, the morning drive to the studio, and even as she worked.

"I'm back." The breezy voice belonging to Rae's store manager preceded by mere seconds Jenna's entrance as she sailed around the partition that separated the studio's work area from the lobby. "Am I late?"

"Uh-uh. Customer's not here yet."

"Good. Thanks for filling in for me." Jenna immediately went to work arranging a cosmetics tray.

"Anytime. What could be more important than Lamaze classes? And if you're willing to step in at the last minute to help your cousin, the least I can do is give you time off."

Jenna wrinkled her nose. "Who'd have thought I'd be playing the man's part?"

"Your cousin's probably just as confused about her part since the untimely departure of her significant other."

"He didn't die. He skipped town. You're right, though. I wouldn't like being in her shoes right now."

The bell on the front counter rang.

"I'll get it," Jenna said. "Now that I'm back, you don't have to hang around unless you want to."

"Thought I'd get some paperwork done as long as I'm here. I'll be in the office."

The moment Rae got settled at the computer, however, Jenna returned.

"My client's here, and I thought you might want to know there's a hunk out front ogling your portrait."

Rae laughed. "And what did this hunk say he wanted?"

"He didn't say, and I didn't ask. From the look on his face, though, I'd guess he wants you. Why don't you go check him out?"

"Why don't I?" Getting up from the desk, Rae slipped her shoes on and headed for the lobby.

Daniel. He stood in front of her picture, gazing up at it as Jenna had described, and something in his expression made her hesitate for a moment before speaking.

"Hello, Daniel."

He turned slowly, grinning as he leaned on the counter that separated them. "Tell me, exactly what does it take to be considered a 'hunk'?"

"What big ears you have, Grandpa," she said, refusing to blush. "Did you come here just to ask that question?"

"Nope." He took her hand in his. "I came to see your portrait, but I hoped to see you, too."

"How did you know I'd be here—oh, I didn't tell you my schedule, did I? Today's a fluke. Most weeks I come in only on Monday and Friday."

"Semi-retirement?"

"Not exactly. The rest of the time I work out of my home office. When the girls moved in with me, I found out the hard way that I'm not a superwoman. The children come first, so I cut back my hours at the studio, moved to a smaller town with a slower pace, and hired a housekeeper. That leaves me nearly enough time and energy to keep up with Kris and Erin."

"Sounds pretty super to me." He gave her hand a gentle squeeze. "In fact, you're the most super woman I've ever known."

This time, she couldn't control the blush she felt creeping up her neck as she looked away from the intense gray eyes that seemed to be able to see into her soul. For a few seconds, she couldn't speak. When she could, she changed the subject.

"What about you? No pilots to train today?"

"Always. As a matter of fact, I should be on my way back to the flight academy."

"Then I'll show you around the studio some other time."

"Oh, well, since I'm already here . . . if it won't take more than a half hour?"

She burst out laughing. "Five minutes would be my guess. Come on back."

He walked around the counter and followed her into the work area.

"We've divided the workroom into two sections to keep the lights from the makeup mirrors from interfering with the photographic lighting and vice versa." To demonstrate, she turned on the lights of one of the large mirrors.

"So here's where the transformations take place."

"It is, indeed," she said, not even trying to conceal her pride as she watched him survey the neat, clean, professional-looking surroundings. "You'd be surprised how often our customers leave with more than a new hairdo and a picture. Appearance has a lot to do with self-esteem, you know."

He gave his heart-stopping half smile. "Maybe I'll get you to make me over."

"I wouldn't change a thing," she said softly as she switched off the lights. With a hand on his arm, she guided him to the other work station. "Here we shoot the photos."

After pausing to watch Jenna set the lighting for her client, they continued to the small office at the rear of the store.

"This is the nerve center of the whole operation, but be careful where you sit. You could find yourself permanently wedged in."

"It's not that small." He looked around. "Just the same, I think I'll stand."

"I was wrong," Rae said with a grin. "The grand tour only took about three minutes."

"Three fascinating minutes."

"Ahem!" They both turned toward Jenna, who spoke from the doorway. "I have everything under control now, Rae, so there's no reason for you to stick around any longer."

Dumbfounded, Rae could only stare at her usually ultra-efficient manager. Jenna couldn't possibly have forgotten Rae's plan to tackle the paperwork.

Stepping in to fill the brief silence, Daniel said, "If you're free for the rest of the afternoon, why don't you come with me?"

Turning her eyes on him, Rae felt as though she were

looking out from the wrong side of the looking glass.
"I thought you had work to do."

He smiled. "You can help me with it."

For the second time in less than a minute, Rae found
herself speechless.

His smile broadened. "Honestly. I could use your
help. Come out to the academy with me. First I'll give
you the three-dollar tour. Then I'll put you to work."

"I have to be home by six-thirty."

"Promise. We'll take your car so you can leave
whenever you want to. I can hitch a ride back later."

Giving her no time to formulate a refusal, Daniel
hustled her out of the studio, and in a few minutes she
found herself southbound on I-35, following Daniel's
directions to the New World Airways Flight Academy.

When they arrived, Daniel quickly checked his office
for messages before beginning the tour. Whatever pre-
conceptions Rae had had of the flight academy, she'd
never imagined its sheer size. That it would require so
much space to train pilots never occurred to her until
she and Daniel began making their way from building
to building, all connected by a labyrinth of corridors
and walkways. And size was but her first revelation.

Everything fascinated her, from the desk where the
trainees checked in each morning to receive their daily
assignments to the classrooms to the computer center,
where several trainees sat, each wearing a headset to
eliminate outside distractions while gazing intently into
a computer monitor.

With instructors and students alike concentrating on
the business of flying airplanes, she and Daniel seemed
to be the only two people in the entire complex not
currently engaged in pilot training. Even the one man
they encountered as they left the computer center was
so absorbed in the material he carried that he merely
glanced up as he passed and muttered, "Hey, Danny
boy," before returning his attention to his papers.

Daniel acknowledged him with a brief nod, but neither man seemed inclined to stop and converse further.

"Danny," Rae said softly. "Is that your nickname?"

"Nope."

"Mac?"

"Uh-uh. But I'll answer to anything *you* call me."

"I rather like Daniel."

One corner of his mouth lifted into a half smile. "He's very glad to know it."

He took her arm and ushered her into a hangarlike enclosure that housed a huge swimming pool and what appeared to be the middle section of an airplane.

"That's the mock-up where the flight attendants train," he explained with a gesture at the truncated plane. "The interior can be configured to match any aircraft we fly. They practice water rescue in the pool."

"Sounds like hard work."

He nodded, and his voice took on a tone that resembled a college lecturer's. "They're highly trained individuals, not simply the glorified waiters and waitresses most people think they are."

"You don't have to play tour guide for me. You forget, I've had the opportunity to see some of them in action."

"Sorry," he said with a self-mocking smile. "And, no, I don't forget. Not ever."

"Daniel . . ."

He shook his head to silence her. "It's okay. If we can't talk about it to each other, who can we talk to?"

They crossed the room to exit through a door that put them on a path to an even larger building, this one filled with several box-shaped devices atop platforms mounted on what appeared to be sets of massive springs and some sort of huge hydraulic jacks.

"Flight simulators."

She nodded as she looked up at the odd-looking boxes.

Pointing across the room, Daniel said, "The one moving is in operation."

"When you're inside, do you feel like you're really in a plane?"

"Come see for yourself." He led her up a staircase to a walkway at the rear of one of the mock aircraft, and after unlocking the door, he motioned her inside.

Entering the simulator was like stepping into a different time and place. The hangar ceased to exist. The cramped airplane cockpit became reality.

"Feel real?" he asked, locking the door behind them.

"Does to me, but you're the expert. Is it authentic?"

"Except for this." He patted a panel of switches and lights on his left. "The instructor sits here and creates all kinds of fun things for the pilot to deal with."

"That's what you do?"

He nodded. "This is where you come in. All this is computer-driven. Last night it went down, and now I have to give it a thorough check to make sure it's operating properly. You game?"

"Oh." Her pulse quickened, and she could almost feel her adrenaline kick in as her excitement mounted. "Of course."

"Then have a seat up front on the left, and we'll see if you can fly this thing."

"Me? You're kidding!"

"Nope. Ever flown a plane before?"

"Not even a kite."

"That's okay. I won't let you crash." He laughed, but the words hung in the air between them. As his smile faded, his tone became subdued. "Not this time."

"If I didn't believe in you, I wouldn't be here."

She took her place in the designated seat, looking around at the incomprehensible array of gauges, switches, and controls while Daniel busied himself at the instructor's panel.

"Those screens are your windows," he said, apparently recovered from his pang of guilt. "Pretty soon I'll have something for you to look at."

The words had barely escaped his lips when a runway appeared in the "windows," enhancing the eerie sense of being out of time and place, and she felt her self-confidence waver. Not until Daniel joined her, taking the other seat, did she regain some of her enthusiasm.

Briefly, he explained how to read the gauges before he said, "Now I'm going to start one engine. Then it will be your turn."

Watching his every move with absolute concentration, Rae felt as well as heard the engine roar to life, and with her heart in her mouth, she repeated the steps he'd just shown her. Miraculously, the second engine started.

"Good." His encouragement, coupled with her initial success, eased her tension somewhat, but not enough to rid her of the knots in her stomach.

"Put your feet on those pedals," Daniel continued. Speaking with quiet assurance, he showed her how to operate each of the controls as she listened with single-minded intensity. "Ready?"

"I don't think so."

"Sure you are. Remember, we won't leave the ground."

Following his directions, she started the plane down the runway, and before she knew it, they were airborne. The already weighted conversation became completely one-sided, with Daniel giving instructions and Rae struggling to comply, until she completed the program and somehow managed to land the plane without losing any major parts. Except her nerve.

"Keep your seat for a minute," he said as he got up to go to the control board. When he returned, he leaned over her to shut down the engines. "That's all there is to it."

Following him to the back of the simulator, she leaned against the wall while she regained her sense of reality.

When he turned toward her, he frowned and reached out to touch her cheek. "You okay?"

"If you don't count a splitting headache and the fact that my knees are so wobbly I can hardly stand."

He chuckled, drawing her into a comforting embrace. "That bad?"

"Something between ecstasy and torture." Glad for his support, she returned his embrace, slipping her arms around him as she rested her head against his chest. "It was such a rush, yet at the same time I felt major-league stupid."

"You did great considering that you got about thirty days of instruction thrown at you in an hour and a half."

"Thirty days?"

"That's how long it takes to put a pilot through the academy—a pilot with considerable experience before he even begins. That help?"

"A little, maybe, in the ego department, but not if you're talking about the meltdown going on in my brain."

"Then how's this?" Gently, he took her face between his hands, smoothing her hair back as he massaged her temples with his thumbs.

His soothing touch brought immediate relief. Closing her eyes, she began to relax as his lightly stroking fingers coaxed the tension from her, and soon her headache faded completely away.

Exactly when his touch changed from one of comfort to a caress, she didn't know, but slowly she became aware that it had grown less therapeutic and more pleasurable. Moving his fingers over her face, he investigated at leisure every curve, every angle, and when he finally tilted her face toward his, she didn't resist.

Nor did she object when his lips took up where his hands had left off. Brushing her face with a series of light kisses, he moved slowly, as if savoring each sensation, as he progressed from her forehead to her eyelids and cheeks to the tip of her nose to her chin—everywhere except where she most wanted his touch. With each tender caress her impatience grew, until finally his lips found hers, putting an end to her frustrated longing.

With a sigh, she tightened her arms around him, and the answering pressure of his embrace drew her even closer, molding her body to his with an urgency that matched her own. No longer light and leisurely, his kiss became more demanding as he took complete possession of her mouth, exploring every hollow, every surface, thrusting into every moist, secret place.

Without leaving the ground, they once more broke the law of gravity. This time, however, instead of hurtling through the sky at breakneck speed in the metal body of a man-made craft pushed along by massive engines, they floated free, alone together in some undefined space ruled by passion. Even after the kiss ended, it took her a few minutes to regain her equilibrium.

"Know how much I wanted to do that last night?" he murmured between ragged breaths.

"I know how much I wanted you to. Why didn't you?"

She could almost feel his irresistible half smile, and she looked up only to discover it poised so near that his breath brushed her face lightly as he spoke.

"Don't know. Maybe I wanted you to want it a little while longer."

"Once kissed, was I not supposed to want any more?"

His smile broadened. "Once kissed, you were supposed to want a lot more. Or did I do something wrong?"

"You didn't do anything wrong," she whispered as she lifted her lips to meet his with an eagerness that more than proved her point.

FOUR

Daniel pulled up in front of Rae's home and parked behind a black Camaro with dealer's tags and a Blackwell Motors decal on the back. Steve's car. Not the most auspicious beginning to a day he'd been counting the hours toward, but at least the weather was cooperating. He glanced up at the sky as he stepped out of his car. Partly sunny. Not too hot for midsummer. Great day for a picnic.

When he opened the gate and started up the walk, however, Kristen and Erin greeted him with frowns and glum-sounding "hellos." Sitting side by side on the top porch step, they didn't resemble, even remotely, two little girls anticipating a pleasant outing.

"Hi," he said, lowering himself onto the step next to them. "Why the gloomy-looking faces? Picnic been canceled?"

"Nope," Kristen answered for both of them, while Erin climbed onto his lap. "We're mad at Auntie Rae."

"Sounds serious."

"She spanked Erin, Mr. Daniel." Kristen spoke the words as if such a heinous offense needed no further explanation.

The younger child, gazing up at him with her most pitiful expression, plopped her thumb into her mouth and nodded as though to confirm the complaint against Rae.

Swallowing to suppress a laugh at such an obvious play for sympathy, he said, "I can't believe Rae would punish either one of you without a reason. Think she might've had one?"

"Erin jumped off the porch again," Kristen said in a disgusted tone.

"Over there." Erin took her thumb out of her mouth long enough to point toward the end of the porch.

He gave a low whistle. "From the railing?"

Both girls nodded.

He surveyed what would have been a six-foot drop straight down. With shrubs and the sloping lawn complicating matters, it would be that much more hazardous. "No wonder she spanked you." He turned the child on his lap to face him. "You could have broken your pretty little neck with a stunt like that."

Kristen nodded knowingly. "That's what Auntie Rae said." She gave an exaggerated sigh. "But Erin just won't listen."

"It's fun," Erin said with a pout.

"That kind of fun could land you in the hospital. Broken bones hurt like anything, and no amount of kissing can make it feel better. If either of you got hurt like that, it would break Rae's heart. She'd blame herself. Believe me, broken arms and legs are no fun, and you wouldn't want to make Rae feel bad, would you?"

"No," both girls agreed, though Erin didn't sound entirely convinced.

"Rae's probably feeling pretty low about the whole thing, too. Know where she is?" he asked, bringing the unpleasant subject to an end.

"In the kitchen," Kristen answered. "Packing the picnic basket."

"Picnic!" Erin shouted as she bounced off his lap and skipped across the porch, the spanking apparently forgotten.

"You can go on inside if you want to." Kristen sighed. "Erin won't get into any more trouble." Her voice dropped almost to a whisper. "I hope."

Daniel chuckled as he got to his feet and brushed the dust from his jeans. "Think I'll do that."

Entering the house, he proceeded straight to the kitchen. As he approached the door, however, the sound of Steve's voice stopped him from opening it.

". . . alone for a long time. You must know how I've come to feel about you."

"Well, I hope I've earned your respect," Rae replied.

"Respect? That's all? After everything we've been through together and all we've shared, it would be only natural for our relationship to develop into something more than that—something stronger and deeper," Steve persisted in a tone that made Daniel's skin crawl. "I thought it had."

"We've certainly seen each other through some difficult times," Rae answered softly. "And, of course, we have the children . . ."

Not wanting to hear the rest of Rae's quietly voiced reply, Daniel knocked loudly as he pushed open the door and walked into the kitchen. "Rae? Oh, hello. Hope I'm not interrupting anything."

"You are," Steve snapped. "You're supposed to knock and wait to be invited before you come charging into somebody else's house, or didn't your mother bother to teach you manners?"

Completely ignoring Steve, Daniel continued speaking to Rae. "The girls told me I'd find you here."

She smiled, her calm demeanor a direct contrast to the anger that marred Steve's features, and her voice reflected her outward composure. "You're just in time to help. Will you put that cooler on the table for me?"

"Sure." He stepped around Steve to lift the insulated box onto the table. "Anything else?"

"Look, Rae," Steve interjected, "sooner or later you're going to have to deal with this."

With a gesture of impatience, she turned to face him. "With what? What is it you want from me?"

"Family loyalty." Scowling, he leaned over the table until his face was only inches from hers. "Nothing I don't have a right to expect, but the way you've been carrying on the past few days makes me wonder if you remember what it means."

"How dare you question me on that!" she said sharply.

"Lately you've been acting like an empty-headed schoolgirl and neglecting your family responsibilities." He turned to glare at Daniel. "He's been filling your head with garbage that's made you forget all about Karen. But remember, you owe her, Rae. And she'd expect you to help her children get what's coming to them."

Her face drained of color as she replied in a deadly quiet tone, "Nobody knows how much I owe Karen better than I do."

Steve's tone moderated, but the piercing stare he fixed on her revealed a vague threat hiding beneath his perfect features. "Just don't forget that when the trial rolls around, and don't even think about selling out to the other side. The girls and I need your support in this."

"I can testify to the facts, that's all." She glanced at Daniel. "I can't alter the truth. No one can."

"So that's how it is. You think I don't see those cozy looks you've been giving each other?" Steve turned his fury on Daniel. "You know exactly how to work her, don't you? Your butt's in a sling, so you figure you'll waltz on over here and romance your way out of it. You'll use a little flattery, a little flirtation, even a hot night or two if that's what it takes to get what you want. Then, after she's saved your bacon in court, you'll disappear so fast her head'll be spinning. I know your type."

Furious, Daniel felt the heat rise in his face as he fought the urge to shove his fist right into the middle of the smug jerk's face, but before his anger had a chance to take over, Kristen and Erin burst through the kitchen door.

"Auntie Rae, Auntie Rae," they squealed in unison. As Steve stormed out of the room, however, they fell silent, staring after their father.

"What is it?" Rae prompted reassuringly.

Kristen recovered first. "Erin promised she won't jump off the porch anymore."

"Nope," Erin agreed.

"Good." Rae knelt to give her nieces each a hug.

Daniel could already feel his blood pressure going down, and the tension eased from Rae's face as she smiled up at him.

"You wouldn't be responsible for this attitude adjustment, would you?" she asked.

"Not me," he answered. "Kris and Erin probably just decided they didn't want to upset you anymore, right?"

He winked at them, and taking their cue, both children nodded.

"Uh-huh," Rae said skeptically. "All on their own?"

"Absolutely," he assured her.

"Absolutely," the girls echoed.

She laughed. "Okay. Then, if everybody's ready, let's get this picnic stuff loaded so we can get going."

"At your service," he volunteered, using his most gallant manner.

He picked up the cooler, and Rae carried the picnic basket, while Kris and Erin ran ahead to open doors for them. After they had all buckled their seat belts, they set off.

Although they covered no more than ten miles, the drive took almost half an hour as they wound their way through the LBJ Grasslands to Black Creek Lake over terrain that made a vehicle such as Rae's necessary. When they arrived, they scouted the area for a shaded picnic table before unloading the food.

"Yummy," Kristen murmured, eyeing the peach cobbler Rae set on the table. "Can we eat now?"

"I suppose," Rae said. "But you have to wait until after lunch to have dessert."

"Aw, do we have to?" Daniel playfully joined the little girls in mild protest, but when Rae gave his hand a light swat, all three gave in.

In spite of their grumbling, however, they ate with such relish that by the time she served the cobbler, no one had room for more than a small helping, and Daniel declined altogether.

"Can we go for a walk now?" Kristen asked as soon as she'd downed her last bite of cobbler.

"Wait until we get the leftovers packed up," Rae answered. "Then we'll go with you."

Kris tried again. "But we won't go very far, and we'll stay away from the water."

"No water," Erin echoed.

"I said to wait." Without raising her voice, Rae managed to convey that further argument would be useless. "This won't take long."

It didn't, and soon, with the impatient children running ahead of them, they set off toward the lake. For a while, they followed the shoreline, but heavy brush impeded their progress, forcing them to turn around and retrace their steps. Such a minor setback hardly bothered the girls at all as they eagerly explored their surroundings. Eventually, though, fatigue slowed them down. By the time they got back to the picnic area, Kristen's feet were dragging, and Erin had cajoled Daniel into carrying her. When Rae spread a blanket in the shade of a large oak tree for them to lie down on, both children promptly fell asleep.

With a yawn, Daniel stretched out on the other end of the blanket. "Nice place," he said as Rae sat down next to him. "I'm surprised more people don't use it. Can't believe we only ran into two other groups here on a Saturday. The park should be packed."

"Even though it's close to town, it's not all that easy to find."

He chuckled. "Or find your way back from. I hope you brought a map—or left a trail of bread crumbs?"

"Oh, no," she exclaimed in mock horror. "I knew I forgot something."

Laughing, he said, "Well, we won't starve, anyway. You brought enough food to feed forty people."

"I wanted to make sure we'd have plenty. Besides, except for spaghetti, I had no idea what you might like."

"What I'd really like is a chance to clear the air about what Steve said this morning," he replied, sobering somewhat as he gazed up at her. "Trying to influence your testimony never occurred to me. Frankly, I don't think anything you can say will have much effect on the outcome of that lawsuit."

"Neither do I. Besides, you don't strike me as the gigolo type." She shrugged. "Don't worry about Steve. He can be hot-tempered at times, and today he got mad because you interrupted our conversation."

"So I gathered." Taking a deep breath, he continued. "While I'm at this, I may as well confess. I overheard you talking right before I barged into your kitchen. The conversation sounded personal. And serious. I guess what I want to know is . . . how serious?"

She sighed. "Pretty serious. I'm helping to raise his children."

"Then how personal? Exclusive?"

"I would say so. Raising children by committee doesn't work very well." She smiled, a teasing glint in her eyes. "Serious and exclusive, but not romantic, if that's what you're getting at. To me, Steve will always be Karen's husband."

Relieved, Daniel breathed deeply. "You have a wicked sense of humor, lady. I felt like a pimply teenager trying to find out if you were going steady."

"Nope," she replied, laughing. "Never have."

"Why not, Rae?" he asked, not joking now. "Why aren't you married with a dozen or so children of your own?"

Her smile took on a wry twist. "Nobody ever asked."

"You're kidding! There can't be that many stupid men in the world. It's not possible."

"Possible and accurate." She shrugged. "Not that it matters much, since I've never known anyone I'd have accepted. Most men who hung around me just wanted to get near Karen. I wanted to be more than a consolation prize for some guy lusting after my sister. What about you? Why don't you have a wife stashed away in a cozy cottage somewhere?"

"Did once. Years ago, in my callow youth, I married a woman I'd known for two months. The marriage lasted slightly longer than the courtship, but in the end, it couldn't withstand the demands of my career."

"Your wife didn't like pilots?"

"On the contrary, she loved them—all of them—one by one. It didn't matter much to her which pilot happened to be passing through town."

Rae looked away, her discomfort apparent. "I had no business asking that sort of thing."

"Why not? I started it, and it doesn't matter." He

lifted his hand to her cheek as he coaxed her to meet his gaze. "It hasn't mattered for a long time."

For a moment she looked as though she intended to speak, but instead, she leaned over and kissed him. Adjusting quickly to her unexpected gesture, he surrendered to her sweet caress, and while the gentle pressure of her lips on his both satisfied and aroused, he didn't try to force the progression prematurely. He let it grow gradually, naturally, as she settled into his arms. Holding her close, he inhaled deeply of her clean, fresh scent, delighting in the feel of her soft, silky hair on his cheek, reveling in her nearness—until he opened his eyes to see Erin peering at him from over Rae's shoulder.

"Hi," Erin said, squatting beside Rae as she watched them intently. "Whatcha doin'?"

Rae's face flushed as she quickly sat up, and when she didn't reply, Daniel answered instead. "Kissing Rae, or rather, she was kissing me."

"Oh." The child paused, tilting her head as if in deep thought before asking, "What for?"

"Now that you're awake," Rae interrupted, "how about some more peach cobbler?"

Jumping up and down, Erin yelled, "Yum. Peaches."

Awakened by the commotion, Kristen sleepily rubbed her eyes and mumbled, "Me, too, please."

"Let's all have some," Rae suggested. Rising, she started over to the picnic table, followed closely by her nieces.

"Not me, thanks," Daniel said, getting up to fold and put away the blanket. By the time he joined them, Rae had regained her composure, and he resisted the urge to tease her about her embarrassment. Instead, he watched her fill paper plates with generous mounds of cobbler as he settled himself beside her on the bench.

Serving the girls and herself, Rae glanced over at him. "Sure you won't have some?"

"No, thanks," he said, unable to suppress a grimace. "I'll pass."

With a little shrug, she dug into her second helping of dessert. "From the look on your face, I'd guess you don't particularly like peach cobbler. As a child, were you attacked by a peach, or something?"

He grinned. "Just about. I grew up on my parents' farm down in Walnut Springs. That's south of Fort Worth, near Glen Rose. And on that farm we had a peach orchard, e-i-e-i-o. To make an already-too-long story longer, one year we harvested a bumper crop of peaches. We picked peaches, peeled peaches, canned peaches, and froze peaches for what must have been the longest growing season on record. All the while, of course, we ate peaches, and ate peaches, and ate peaches. After that summer, I was never able to look a peach in the pit again. Tragic, huh?"

"Poor baby," Rae teased, smiling. Reaching into the picnic basket, she pulled out a bag of fresh fruit. "Maybe you can find something in there that doesn't grow on your parents' farm."

"As a matter of fact, we've never grown bananas," he said, selecting one from the bag.

Rae turned her attention to her cobbler. She lifted her fork, then paused for a moment before setting it back down. Pushing her plate away from her, she said, "Hand me one of those apples."

Laughing, Daniel tossed her the shiny red fruit. "Sorry I ruined your dessert for you."

"Never mind. It was my second helping," she said, biting into the crunchy apple.

While they ate, they fell silent, but it was a companionable silence. Watching Rae, Daniel marveled at how quickly she'd managed to restore to him an inner peace he'd thought he would never again know.

He was still pondering how she worked her healing magic when they repacked the truck and headed home.

He didn't often have the opportunity to enjoy a day like the one drawing to an end, and reluctant to relinquish the warm feelings generated by the pleasant afternoon shared with Rae and the children, he wanted somehow to push back the approaching twilight that signaled the end of their outing.

Arriving at Rae's house, he stalled for time, volunteering to unload the truck and unpack the leftovers while Rae straightened up the kitchen. They'd just finished when Kris and Erin came in, each carrying a handful of mail.

Annoyance crossed Rae's face, settling in her eyes, and her voice reflected her irritation when she said, "You know you're not supposed to even open the gate unless a grown-up is with you."

As usual, Kristen acted as spokesperson for both children. "We didn't Auntie Rae."

Rae knelt to give each girl a direct look in the eye. "Then how did you get the mail from a box that's outside the fence?"

"I boosted Erin up, and she leaned over to get it," Kristen almost whispered, her eyes wide. "But we didn't go out of the yard."

Rae sighed deeply and dropped her head into her hands for a moment. When she looked back up at her nieces, she said, "It'll be a miracle if you two survive childhood." Her tone changed to one of authority. "New rule. Nobody boosts anybody over the fence ever again for anything, and no getting the mail unless an adult is with you. Is that clear?"

"Yes, ma'am," they said in unison, but while Erin wore a defiant pout, Kristen appeared genuinely contrite.

"Now, go upstairs and wash up. We'll have an early supper, if you have room for anything else after eating all that cobbler, then baths and bed. You've had quite a day." She drew them both into a hug, giving each a kiss on the cheek before sending them on their way.

Daniel reached down to help her to her feet. With a sigh of resignation, she shook her head, and he couldn't help chuckling as he took her into his arms and kissed her forehead.

She accepted his embrace, resting her head on his shoulder for a few minutes before drawing away.

"Better?" he asked.

She nodded. "Sometimes it seems like children can find a million ways to get around any rule that an adult can come up with."

"They're good kids. I don't think they'd upset you on purpose."

"Kristen wouldn't, but Eri—" She shrugged. "That child would try anything once, and if she liked it and thought she'd get away with it, she'd do it again."

"High-spirited."

"Or something." Changing the subject, she asked, "Why don't you stay for dinner, or have you had enough of us for one day?"

"Not at all. Today's the best time I've had in ages, but I don't want to outstay my welcome."

"You couldn't," she assured him as she gave him a wry smile. "We're having leftovers from our picnic for dinner, though, so consider yourself warned."

"A buffet? Good idea. Now I can sample some of the stuff I didn't have room for at lunch," he replied, teasing.

"Next time," she threatened playfully, "you get a single bologna sandwich, and not one thing with it."

He laughed, and she laughed with him until she picked up the mail the girls had brought in. Abruptly, her laughter stopped, and her smile changed to a frown as she set all but the top letter on the table. Silently, she ripped open the envelope, read the contents, and shoved it into her jeans pocket. Without comment, she removed the rest of the mail to the hall table. When she returned to the kitchen, no trace of anything amiss remained.

Working together, they set out the picnic food, and the girls, with clean faces and hands, joined them for the meal. While Erin chattered away as usual, Kristen remained subdued. Even the prospect of a bit more peach cobbler didn't interest her.

"Are you feeling okay?" Rae asked, reaching over to touch the child's forehead.

"Yes, ma'am," Kristen whispered, but tears spilled from her eyes and ran down her cheeks. "I didn't mean to be bad." The moment the words cleared her mouth, she burst into sobs.

"I know, baby." Rae picked her up and, with Erin trotting along behind them, headed for the back stairs. Over her shoulder, Rae called to Daniel, "Excuse us, please."

Daniel watched them go as he began clearing the table. If not for their obvious devotion to each other, he would never have pegged two such different little girls as sisters. Even in the short time he'd known them, he could tell that Erin was the one perpetually on the lookout for mischief to get into, while Kristen, who always tried so hard to live up to expectations of her, often paid the price for her sister's antics. Super-sensitive to Rae's slightest displeasure, Kris took even the mildest scolding hard. The poor kid had a tough road ahead of her. He knew from experience that nobody ever attained perfection, no matter how diligently he worked toward that goal.

"You didn't have to do that," Rae said as she entered the kitchen.

Closing the dishwasher, Daniel turned to give the table one last wipe. "It's the least I could do. How's Kris?"

"Exhausted. She takes everything so much to heart. I try to be careful, but sometimes . . ."

"She's in for some tough times," he agreed. "You haven't had the best of evenings, either, between dealing with her hurt feelings and the letter that upset you earlier."

Her eyes widened as she said, "You noticed."

"Not because you didn't cover it well. I don't want to interfere, but if it's anything I can help with . . ."

"My parents are coming for a visit. I don't see how you or anyone else can stop that."

FIVE

Surprise flashed briefly in Daniel's eyes "Sounds like you're anything but happy about it."

Rae slumped against the door, her resilience momentarily depleted. "If you're up to hearing a long, sad story, I'll put the coffee on."

"Let me do that. You need a break." After guiding her to a chair, he set about preparing coffee for the two of them. When it was ready, they settled in the living room with their steaming mugs.

Sinking into the comfortable sofa cushions, she reached into her pocket to retrieve the envelope. "Here," she said, holding it out to him, "you can start with this."

He unfolded the single page, and as he read the businesslike letter, a curious frown creased his brow. Any questions he might have had, however, he kept to himself.

"Short and to the point, isn't it?" she said when he returned it to her without comment.

"For a letter from your parents, it sounds kind of . . . cool." He spoke slowly, as though choosing his words carefully. "I can't help wondering why, but if you don't want to talk about it . . ."

"Not much to tell." She slipped her shoes off and tucked her feet underneath her. "It's always been that way between us—at least, since they moved to Africa. You see, Nick and Edie, my parents, do volunteer work for Ease Human Suffering. Ever heard of it?"

He nodded slowly. "On those TV commercials, the ones that run all the time late at night. They distribute food in famine areas, don't they?"

"Yeah," she answered, staring into the black liquid in her cup. "EHS does a lot more than supply food, though. They build roads, dig wells, provide seed for planting, or whatever else the local population needs to help them become self-sufficient—including educating the children. That's where Nick and Edie come in. They teach."

"Noble occupation."

"Well, maybe. Unfortunately, they already had two daughters when they joined EHS, and they were sent into the middle of a civil war that's been going on for years. It's so bad, even charity workers become targets from time to time. Anyway, raising children under those conditions was out of the question, so they left us behind. I'd barely turned six. Karen was eight. They only came back for occasional visits, and for a long time Karen and I wondered what was wrong with us. We were too young to understand about war and politics and the like. We only knew our parents didn't want us anymore."

He took a sip from his cup, his features unreadable. After a few minutes, however, he asked, "Who'd they leave you with? I mean, they didn't abandon you to the state, did they?"

She couldn't suppress a grim smile. "They left us in the custody of our grandmother, Eleanor Wyatt, as in *the* Wyatts of Boston, but she doesn't spend much time at the family estate in the city. Summers she goes to her vacation home on Cape Cod, near Hyannis, and most winters to the Riviera. My father, Nicholas Layton Garrett the Third, comes from equally impressive stock. Layton Industries in New Hampshire.''

"Whew!" It came out a long, low whistle. "That sure raised a lump in the throat of this Texas country boy. Better check.'' He took her hand and placed it on his chest. "My heart still beating?"

His playful reaction lightened her dark mood, and when he made no move to release her hand, she entwined her fingers with his. "Something tells me you didn't expect a poor-little-rich-kid story."

"As a matter of fact, I didn't," he agreed. "The kind of money you're talking about is usually easy to spot, but you don't exactly flaunt your . . . well, your . . . affluence, if you'll pardon the understatement. Your accent doesn't help much, either. Not dyed-in-the-wool Texas, but Boston?''

"No," she said, unable to keep a note of self-mockery out of her voice. "It's that rich-bitch accent you get from attending only *the* most exclusive boarding schools."

"I never said that."

"You didn't have to. I know it. Karen had it, too. We could hardly have avoided that oh-so-proper diction since we spent virtually every day of our lives, from the time Nick and Edie went on their merry way until we graduated from college, at one school or another."

"Thought you lived with your grandmother," he said, sounding thoroughly puzzled.

"Eleanor was our legal guardian, but we never lived with her, unless you count the six days we stayed at her house before the start of the term at our first boarding school. After that, we didn't have a home. Not even the illusion of one. Between terms, we were shuffled off to camp. Holidays, we stayed at school, if it remained open. If it closed, we were packed off to Boston, where we celebrated with the servants until we got old enough that having us around made them nervous. From then on, it was just the two of us. Not exactly tragic. We never lacked anything material. And, of course, we had each other.''

"That's why you're determined to give Kris and Erin as normal a home life as possible.''

"I want them to have a sense of security at least," she said, swallowing unshed tears "Every child needs somebody who loves and believes in them no matter what, and if I can help it, my nieces will never have to wonder why nobody wanted them.''

Without a word, he took her coffee mug from her and set both their cups aside. Then, reaching out to draw her into his arms, he held her gently as she settled into his welcome embrace.

After a while, she said, "I don't want Nick and Edie breezing into town and confusing the girls with their warped set of values. Karen didn't want them around her children, and if she'd lived, I don't think the past two years would have changed her mind. But I'm still not sure how to handle this. I'll probably leave it up to Steve.''

"That'll simplify matters," Daniel said sharply, but his tone moderated as he went on. "But don't the girls ask about their grandparents?''

"Not so far." She sighed. "Lucky for me, I suppose.''

"Yeah. You'd think they'd have asked a million questions after the funeral, meeting their grandparents for the first time and all.''

"Nick and Edie didn't come back for Karen's funeral. They sent a lovely condolence card, though.'' Trying to disguise her bitterness would have been a waste of time. She would never forgive Nick and Edie for caring so little for Karen that they hardly bothered to acknowledge her death.

Daniel ran a soothing hand over Rae's hair. "Guess money really can't buy happiness. No wonder you don't make a big deal about being so . . . rich."

"Uh-oh. Brace yourself for another shock." She looked up at him, watching him closely as she prepared to set the record straight. "I'm not rich. By the time I completed college, Karen and I had already decided to go into business together, and we wanted to make it on our own, so as soon as I finished school, we cut all ties to our family."

"At least you had capital."

"No, we didn't," she snapped. "We started with a bank loan, like everybody else does." She paused and took a deep breath. "I didn't mean to bite your head off, but you hit a raw nerve. It drives me crazy that people always assume we used family money. I'll admit, getting a loan was probably easier for us than for most people starting their own business, but we did get it, and we paid it back out of profits. We disposed of our trust funds before we even applied to the bank. Sorry, but I'm just a normal, everyday, working-class joe, trying to make a living."

"Don't say anything else, Rae. My heart can't take it," he teased. "First you make me believe I've got my arms around more money than most people earn in a lifetime, and then, in the blink of an eye, it's all gone. How much can a man be expected to take?"

"And I thought you liked me for myself," she replied, unable to keep a note of apprehension out of her voice. She'd been disappointed by more than one man who hadn't been able to see her through the dollar signs in his eyes.

With a hand under her chin, Daniel tilted her face toward his until their eyes met. "In the first place, I didn't know anything about your family until this minute. Second, you're more important to me than any amount of money. In fact, you're so near perfect, it scares the hell out of me."

Rae laughed, releasing the tension that had developed while she'd talked about her childhood. "But if I were perfect, I'd have forgiven my parents a long time ago."

"Mm-hmm. Fortunately, you're as human as the rest of us," he murmured, bending down to brush her lips with his. "Or else I'd be afraid to do something like this."

His arms tightened around her, his usual gentleness nowhere in evidence as his mouth found hers, hungrily parting her lips beneath his. Searching and demanding, his tongue moved inside to engage hers in a hot, wildly exciting duel that stole her breath away. Desire blazed to life. Caught off guard by the depth and intensity of the feelings that threatened to consume her, she struggled to maintain her mental balance, but it was no use. The room was spinning around her, and he gave her no chance to recover her composure as he continued his relentless assault on her senses, stripping her of self-control.

Her hands, almost of their own accord, began to roam over his body. Gliding over the soft cotton of his shirt, they explored the corded muscles beneath the fabric, and when a groan of pleasure rumbled deep in his throat, they became even more insistent in their need to seek out every intimate detail they could find.

His hands were busy, too. One arm held her tightly to him, while his free hand began a separate journey. Beginning at her throat, it traveled a wonderfully roundabout route down to her breast, where, stroking and teasing, it sent delicious fingers of pure pleasure darting through her body. Helpless to fight it, she gave in completely to the urgency building in her, and when his lips followed the path of his hands, she didn't object.

Not until she felt him tugging at the buttons of her blouse did she wake from her passion-induced stupor.

"No," she gasped in a voice that sounded strange even to her.

Daniel stopped immediately and pulled away from her, his agitation apparent as he ran a hand through his hair and moved to the edge of the sofa.

Struggling to button her blouse with fingers that refused to do as her brain commanded, she managed an unsteady "I . . . I'm sorry."

"Yeah, guess we both are," he said, his voice hoarse with barely controlled emotion. "Do me a favor, Rae. Next time you decide you don't want to play the game, call a halt a little earlier in the action, okay?"

"It's not a game to me," she said quietly, making every effort to rid her voice of its telltale tremble. "But thanks for filling me in on the rules. I wouldn't want to get confused, any more than I'd want the girls to be confused if they woke up and came looking for me and found us . . ." Her words dwindled off.

He said nothing. Getting up from the sofa, he walked slowly over to the front door, pausing there for a long moment before he turned around to face her. "So how do you feel about big, dumb jerks?" he asked in a tone that reflected self-reproach.

Mollified somewhat by his unspoken apology, she suppressed a smile and said calmly, "Depends on the jerk in question."

He opened his mouth as if to speak, but instead he let out a long sigh as he leaned against the doorjamb. "I'm sorry, Rae. I didn't mean it the way it sounded. It's not a game to me, either. Hell, I don't even know where that came from."

"It's not all your fault." She went over to stand beside him. "We let things get a little out of control, and as for Kris and Erin, well, neither of us gave them much thought."

The corner of his mouth lifted in a half smile as he took her hands in his, drawing her so close she could feel his warmth, though their bodies didn't quite touch. "Guess we'll have to be more careful next time." He leaned down and kissed her lightly. "But for now, I've about used up all my willpower. It's time I got going."

Reluctantly, she walked him out onto the porch. "After spending the whole day with you, I shouldn't complain because you have to leave. Makes me sound possessive."

"Yeah," he agreed before breaking into a grin. "I kind of like that. Be home tomorrow?"

"Barring emergencies."

"Then I'll give you a call." Taking her face between his hands, he kissed her gently before he left.

As promised, he phoned many times over the next few days. And she didn't hesitate to call him for support when her parents arrived in Fort Worth.

"I realize," she muttered unhappily into the telephone, "that asking you to run interference between me and my parents isn't the most attractive invitation you'll ever get, but I can't face the thought of spending the evening alone with them. If you'll have dinner with us, I promise I'll make it up to you."

"You don't have to bribe me. Just tell me when and where."

His soothing voice washed over her, and his calm assurance steadied her nerves.

"Tonight?"

"Where should I pick you up?"

"Why don't I meet you in town somewhere?"

"My place?"

"Fine," she agreed. "About eight—and, Daniel, this means more to me than I can say. Thanks."

"No problem. I'll expect the same from you when my parents come to town."

"Deal. It couldn't possibly be any more nerve-racking than this."

"I'll tell them you're looking forward to it."

"No, I didn't mean—"

His deep, rich laugh stopped her.

"I know," he said, still chuckling. "I was teasing, sweetheart. Thought it might get your mind off your problems for a little while."

"Oh." She paused. "It worked. For a few minutes there, I couldn't think about anything except the lousy impression your parents would have of me."

"That's one thing you don't have to worry about. They'll love you as much as I do. See you tonight."

Only after he hung up did the import of his words hit her. When realization finally dawned, wondering exactly how he meant it kept her preoccupied for the rest of the day. As she drove into Fort Worth, however, anxiety returned, and by the time she arrived at Daniel's apartment, she desperately needed the quiet, unquestioning support she knew he would provide.

Wearing nothing but jeans, he answered her ring. "Come on in."

"I'm early. Sorry," she managed, struggling to tear her eyes away from the inviting expanse of chest that confronted her.

"No problem." He brushed his lips over hers, drawing her into a reassuring hug. "Make yourself at home while I get dressed."

She nodded, but, reluctant to release him, she slid her hands slowly down his chest as he drew away from her.

"Ahh, sweetheart," he murmured, covering her hands with his. "I gotta get some clothes on, or we'll never get to the restaurant."

"Good idea. Let's not go."

He lifted her hands to his lips and kissed each one. "It'll be okay. I won't be long."

As he disappeared into the next room, she resisted the urge to follow him, contenting herself, instead, with a restless look around his condominium. Beautiful place, though somewhat impersonal. White from the walls to the plush ultramodern furnishings, with a splash of black thrown in here and there as if to ensure against snow blindness, the too-large rooms had a lonely feel to them. Even the few evident attempts at individuality did little to add warmth. On the contrary, they seemed totally out of place, as if by making the changes he'd upset some obscure balance.

"Not much like your home," he commented from the bedroom doorway.

"It's beautiful." She turned to discover him completely transformed, an imposing figure dressed in a dark blue suit. "And so, by the way, are you."

Laughing, he crossed the room to where she waited. "Then we're going to knock everybody's eyes out, lady, because you look gorgeous. Now, let's go make all the other men in the city wish they were me, at least for tonight."

"I don't imagine many women would mind changing places with me, either," she teased back, grateful for his efforts to lighten her mood. She paused to take a deep breath and let it out slowly. "All right, I guess I'm ready."

He took her hand, tucking it into the crook of his arm. "Where are we off to?"

"Marseilles."

Chuckling, he said, "The restaurant?"

She forced a smile at his attempt to ease the tension. "And if I'd meant the city?"

"We'd go. Airline employee's pass, remember?"

For a moment the idea sounded irresistibly tempting, but in the end, her sense of responsibility won out. "I suppose we should stick with the restaurant for tonight. Next time we'll try the city."

"Don't think for a minute that I'll forget your promise," he said as they left the apartment. "I'm going to hold you to it."

"One ordeal at a time, okay?"

He leaned over to kiss her cheek. "You certainly know how to keep a man in touch with reality."

Tears stung her eyes. "I can't seem to say anything right tonight. It's just . . ."

Pausing beside his car, he took her into his arms. "Rae, why let this thing tie you in knots? We're going to have dinner with your parents—"

"Don't call them that."

"With Nick and Edie, then. What can happen? We'll eat, we'll talk, and the minute you want to, we'll leave."

"And you'll be there."

"I'll always be there."

"I know how childish this looks to you. But every time they show up, they bring back memories I don't want to have to deal with anymore, and they stir up so much anger. I've tried to put it behind me, but honestly, I think it would have been easier if they'd never come back from Africa at all. Their visits never accomplished anything except to remind Karen and me that we were unwanted. To you, it's one dinner. For me, it's like revisiting every painful detail from my childhood."

"Then maybe it's time to face it and put it out of your life so it can't come back to haunt you," he said soothingly as he ran his fingertips along her cheek.

"Don't you think I've tried?"

"Sure, but let's try again. What harm can it do?"

Let's, he'd said. Let *us*. He sounded as if he planned to remake her whole life, and if he wanted to attempt it, why not let him? What, besides loneliness and resentment, did she have to lose? And she had everything to gain.

"Thank you, Daniel," she whispered, her strength restored. "I'll be all right now."

"Good." He opened the car door for her, and when she got in, he leaned down to kiss her cheek. "Actors say they deal with stage fright by pretending everybody else is sitting on a toilet. We could try that."

The thought of Nick and Edie in that position made her smile, but when he'd settled himself behind the wheel, she said, "I don't think they ever go."

He laughed, and the deep, familiar sound enveloped her in its protective warmth. "We'll see."

Arriving at their destination, Daniel turned his car over to the valet and, with a reassuring smile, ushered her through the door of the plushly appointed restaurant. Though the place was tastefully decorated, Rae found the dark wood paneling of the entryway oppressive. When the maître d' directed them into the pale-green-and-cream dining room, however, the atmosphere lightened somewhat—until she caught sight of her parents.

At her first glimpse of Edie, she barely suppressed a gasp. She'd forgotten how closely Karen had resembled their mother. Physically. No one who had known Rae's sister would confuse her warmth with Edie's icy perfection. Still, the superficial likeness was stunning.

"Hello," Rae said coolly, after the maître d' had directed her and Daniel to her parents' table.

"Darling," her mother replied, lifting a flawless cheek as if expecting a kiss. "How lovely to see you."

Ignoring Edie's gesture, Rae also managed to evade her father's embrace by offering her hand when he stood and moved toward her. "Nick, Edie." She began introductions as they seated themselves. "I'd like you to meet Daniel MacKay."

"MacKay," Edie repeated. "I don't believe I know that name."

Rae could almost feel smoke rising from the top of

her head as she watched Edie's once-over and perfunctory dismissal of Daniel. Her father's uninterested nod heightened her anger.

Before she could voice her resentment, however, Daniel grinned and said, "No reason why you should. I come from a long line of unknowns. Unless you ever find yourselves in Walnut Springs, Texas. We MacKays are pretty well known thereabouts."

Rae's anger ebbed, and she had to smile. She could hardly keep from bursting into laughter. She'd never heard anyone address any of her family members with such irreverence. She herself had certainly never dared. Clearly, Daniel could take care of himself.

Edie examined Daniel with far greater interest than she'd shown at first, while Nick, looking somewhat taken aback, replied, "We seldom visit Texas. If our daughters hadn't settled in Fort Worth, I'm afraid we would never have traveled down here at all."

"Lucky for you it worked out this way." Daniel continued speaking politely, but with none of the awe usually reserved for those whose bank accounts eclipsed the annual budgets of some countries. "Otherwise you might've missed seeing some of the most beautiful countryside in the world."

"Speaking of traveling," Rae interjected, feeling more relaxed than she had thought possible, "you must have spent some time in New York, or is that haircut the fashion in the African bush this year, Edie?"

"Oh, do you like it, darling?" Edie asked, turning to show off the style to its best advantage. "Philippe created it especially for me."

"As usual, he's done a wonderful job. I hope it won't be too hard keeping it trimmed when you return home." Although Rae tried, she wasn't entirely successful at ridding her voice of a sardonic undertone. "You apparently did some shopping, too. That dress is stunning."

"One tries not to become too outdated." Edie responded to the compliment with obvious relish. "We stayed two weeks in New York. Rushing here and there, seeing to everything. Hair, nails, updating our wardrobes, not to mention doctors and dentists and such. Darling, it was mad but quite marvelous."

A lift of Daniel's eyebrow kept Rae from issuing a sharp retort, and as they placed their dinner orders, she began to believe that getting through the evening without a major disagreement might be possible after all. She could deal with the minor friction as long as the conversation remained on an impersonal level. Her optimism lasted through the appetizer course and until their entrees had been served.

"Well, darling, when do we get to meet those two adorable little girls of yours?" Edie asked, sinking her fork into her lobster thermidor.

"Kristen and Erin are Karen's daughters, or had you forgotten?" Rae's hands clenched involuntarily as the tension she'd been fighting all evening came rushing back. "I had no idea you'd want to see them."

"Why else would we have come all the way down here?" Nick asked, sipping at his wine.

"Certainly not to see me." Rae made no attempt to conceal the sarcasm in her words.

Edie reached over to pat her hand. "Of course we wanted to see you, dear. We always enjoy visiting with you."

"That's why you drop in so often, I imagine."

"Our work keeps us away," Nick said in the tone he usually reserved for the voice-overs of the numerous solicitation ads their organization ran endlessly on late-night television. "We've had to make certain sacrifices over the years, it's true. Compared to the enormous contribution we make toward improving the quality of life for literally millions of less fortunate people, however, they've been worth it."

"Honestly, dear," Edie said, "you're not a child anymore. You're nearly thirty. By now you should be able to understand why we must live out of the country."

"My name is Rae, in case you've forgotten that, too," she said, dropping any pretense of cordiality as she looked her mother straight in the eye. "And I'm thirty-five, but we won't dwell on the details, since you'd have to admit your own age. And believe me, I understand better than you can imagine why you've lived in Africa all these years. Setting all that aside, though, I'm curious to know why it's taken you so long to develop an interest in Kristen and Erin. They're three and five now, yet you've never wanted to see them before."

"My dear, they are our family," Edie said, looking at Rae as if she'd gone mad.

"No." With effort, Rae kept her voice down, but the turmoil raging within pushed her to the edge of control. "They're not Wyatts or Laytons. Kris and Erin are two nice, normal little girls. They won't ever be burdened by those absurd 'family' ties—not if I can help it. I won't let you turn them into the kind of one-dimensional, globe-trotting socialites who know all of the 'right' places, all of the 'right' people, and all of the 'right' things to say and do." She paused, struggling to maintain some semblance of composure. "But if you promise not to upset them, I'll think about letting you see them for a short visit, even though I don't think Karen would have allowed it."

"She most certainly would not have," Nick agreed. "She refused us access to her daughters once before. Your sister was a very bitter woman, Iraina."

Sitting on the edge of her seat, Rae clutched the table so hard that she wouldn't have been surprised to see a piece of it break off in her hands. "Any bitterness you thought you saw in Karen was just your own guilt at abandoning her. But in spite of the poor example you set, she was a warm, loving mother. Don't you dare say another word against her. I won't have it.''

Edie put down her fork and stared curiously at Rae. "Relax, darling. We would never speak ill of your sister. Karen was our daughter, and her death grieved us deeply."

"Oh, yes, thanks for the card." She couldn't stop the words from slipping out.

"We aren't going to get past this resentment of yours, are we?" Edie continued. "All I can say in our defense is that we loved Karen as we know you did. Your father simply meant to point out that Karen wasn't a saint. We know how you adored her, dear, but perhaps it's time you opened your eyes to a few of her imperfections. Such single-minded glorification of her memory can't be healthy."

Rae leapt to her feet, upsetting her water glass, and tears of anger clouded her vision. "How dare you criticize Karen? She was only eight when you left. What could you possibly know about the person she became? I'll tell you this much. She was worth ten of the pair of you."

Vaguely, she became aware of the damp spot slowly spreading across the skirt of her dress, and although a bevy of white-coated attendants flitted around her, the black rage that had taken complete possession of her senses prevented her from understanding their significance. Shaking with uncontrollable anger, she could only wonder if they'd come to take her away to a place where people didn't so easily lose command of themselves, until she felt a strong, supportive arm around her shoulders.

"It's okay, sweetheart." Daniel's soothing voice reached through the thickening fog to her. "Let's go home."

SIX

Slowing for a traffic light, Daniel glanced over at Rae. Huddled in the passenger's seat of his car, clinging to his hand as if her life depended on it, she stared out the window, apparently oblivious to her surroundings.

He'd thought himself prepared for their dinner with Nick and Edie, but he hadn't anticipated anything like Rae's total loss of control. It had caught him completely off guard. Until the moment she had exploded at her parents, she'd given no clue that an eruption was imminent. On the contrary, she had seemed to be handling the situation well in spite of the friction grating beneath the surface. In a classic example of appearances deceiving, she'd fooled him completely.

Finally she spoke. "How bad was it?" she asked in a thin, remote voice that barely rippled the silence in the small car.

"Not too bad," he said quietly. "Probably feels worse than it was."

She closed her eyes, leaning back against the headrest. "Did I . . . what happened?"

He lifted her icy hand to his cheek, holding it there

in an attempt to restore some of its warmth. "You don't remember?"

"Just screaming at them. Something about Karen."

"No screaming, but you said some pretty harsh things to your par—to Nick and Edie." He let go of her hand while he turned into the parking lot of his condominium. After pulling into his space, he walked around to help her out of the car, and together they went inside the building. Closing the door of his apartment behind them, he said nothing as he gathered her into his arms.

For several minutes she, too, refrained from speaking, snuggling into his embrace as if trying to hide from the unpleasantness that had occurred. At last, however, she whispered, "I'm sorry. I shouldn't have dragged you into that . . . that awful scene. I knew it would happen. Something always does when Nick and Edie show up. I just wish I'd kept you out of it."

He guided her to the sofa, taking a seat beside her. "Don't apologize. I'm glad you thought of me when you needed someone. Surprised me a little, though. I mean, you talked about bad feelings between you and your parents, but I had no idea how deep they ran."

"I don't like to talk about it," she explained, embarrassment shading her tone. "Besides, I thought things might not get so out of hand if you were there. Sorry again."

"No problem. But now that we're alone, maybe you could fill in some of the details. Like what it was that got you so upset."

Wide-eyed, she stared at him as though she couldn't believe he had to ask. "Didn't you hear what they said about Karen?"

"Well . . ." Looking down, he took her hand between his and gently stroked each finger, stalling as he tried to formulate his response. Finally, unable to come up with anything better, he said, "Edie said Karen might not have been a saint, and frankly, it didn't sound all that bad to me.''

"You didn't know her," she snapped defensively.

"No, I didn't." He leaned over to give her a quick kiss on the cheek. "And since we didn't have much of a chance to eat earlier, why don't I go see what I can rustle up?"

He stood and walked slowly into the kitchen. Clearly, she had left out some of the details when she'd related the story of her childhood. The Rae he knew wouldn't fly off the handle like that without provocation, yet nothing he'd heard or seen could account for her flare-up.

He checked his kitchen supplies. It would have to be omelets, but he doubted that Rae would mind or even notice the meager fare. Cracking eggs into a bowl, a task he'd performed so often he no longer had to think about it, he let his mind drift.

Nick and Edie had looked as shocked as he was by Rae's reaction to the suggestion that Karen might have had faults. Obviously, Rae believed her sister free of such human frailties. She hadn't been, though, and when Nick had first broached the subject, Daniel thought he'd intended to enlighten Rae about some of Karen's less admirable qualities—qualities he himself had only recently become aware of through the attorneys handling the lawsuit Steve had filed. Common sense eventually ruled out that idea. Nick couldn't possibly know the facts. Few did.

Even so, tonight Daniel had twice witnessed Rae stoutly, if somewhat blindly, defend her sister against fairly mild criticism. He didn't want to be around when she found out the truth. Yet how could he let her hear it from strangers in open court?

"Daniel," she said quietly from the doorway, "can you stand another apology?"

Leaning against the doorjamb with her eyes fixed on

the floor, she looked utterly defeated, and he set aside
the bowl full of the eggs he'd been beating and reached
out to draw her into a comforting hug.

"I thought you could use a few minutes alone, that's
all," he said soothingly.

"To get my brain back in working order?" she
asked, regret overriding her attempt at humor.

"To regain some perspective."

"If that's possible," she said with a sigh. "When it
comes to Nick and Edie, my perspective's all warped."

He pulled out a chair for her before returning his
attention to the egg mixture. "Being an incredibly perceptive man, I managed to pick up on that. Body lan-
guage, I guess."

Just when he thought he would never see her smile
again, she laughed, and her laughter brought relief from
the tension that had been building ever since she had
received her parents' letter.

"You're right, you know," she conceded, the smile
fading from her lips. "Nick and Edie didn't say anything so bad, but coming from them, even the slightest
criticism of Karen is enough to make my blood boil.
She never got over their leaving the way they did, and
yet she tried her best to keep it from affecting me. She
made sure I had somebody to count on, somebody
who'd always be there for me."

Tears choked her voice, and she paused for a moment. When she'd recovered her composure, she went
on. "Griping about the choices Nick and Edie made so
long ago sounds petty, I know. Especially coming from
someone like me. When you think about all the people
who have to struggle every day just to stay alive, the
problems of two little rich girls don't count for much.
But that doesn't mean our needs weren't just as real to
us. And don't get me wrong, it's not EHS I'm com-
plaining about, or even my parents' decision to volun-

teer. It's the way they wear it like a banner and crow about the sacrifices they've made that gets to me.

"At first, when they still had some enthusiasm for the work, they might've lived for a while in a hut in a small village somewhere. Who knows how long the idealism lasted? Now they concentrate on fund-raising, and for as long as I can remember, they've taught only a couple of English classes a week at Ease Human Suffering's headquarters in Addis Ababa—when they're actually *in* Africa. Most of the time they travel.

"For their classes, they fly back and forth between the city and their home in the countryside, and in the few pictures I've seen, the house looks at least three times larger than mine. It's also fully staffed, down to a private security force and an airfield out in back so they can import whatever they want or make a quick getaway, if it comes to that."

Without comment, he sliced the Spanish omelet he'd made into two pieces, slid half onto a plate, added a couple of hot rolls, and set the dish down in front of her, along with a steaming hot cup of tea. "That changes the picture some," he said, preparing a plate for himself. "Sure doesn't conjure up images of civil war."

"There really has been a lot of fighting in that region, and sometimes it includes kidnapping and murder. If the chances of that were high, though, odds are Nick and Edie would've found another cause a long time ago. They're survivors, and you'll notice they've managed to be out of the country during the current crisis. My guess is they got bored. Saving the world sounded romantic. Raising children, even with an army of hired hands to do all the work, was dull by comparison. So they left. They stayed there because they like being thought of as martyrs, but believe me, they've never missed a season on the Riviera or wherever their crowd gathers."

He reached over to give her hand a squeeze. "I think I understand."

"But I ought to be able to get past it? Well, I try. But when they start in on Karen, my self-control flies out the window."

"I sensed that," he said dryly.

Again she smiled. "This is really good," she said, swallowing another bite of omelet.

Accepting the change of subject, he replied, "My one and only culinary success story."

"But man cannot live by omelet alone."

"You'd be surprised how long a man can survive on eggs. I must've eaten a ton of 'em while I was on suspension."

The light that had begun to flicker in her eyes dimmed. Reaching over, she covered his hand with hers. "Wish I'd been there for you."

Raising her hand to his face, he touched his lips gently to her palm and murmured, "You were."

Without another word, he got up and began clearing away their dirty dishes. With Rae's help, the chores didn't take long, and they soon had the kitchen in order. As he straightened up from wiping the table, she stepped behind him and began to massage his back, her fingers proceeding directly to the spot where the pain was centered.

"This where it hurts?" she asked, moving her hands methodically over the tense muscles.

"Oh, yeah." He sighed, standing absolutely still while she coaxed the pain from his body. "How'd you know my back was acting up again?"

She hesitated briefly before answering. "I'm not sure, but it started to bother you while you were cooking, didn't it?"

Turning around, he took her into a tight hug. "Not many people would notice something like that, especially after an evening like the one you had."

"Not many people would suffer in silence while they listened to me complain about my parents," she replied, sliding her arms around him to continue the back rub.

"Guess that makes us even." He chuckled as he reached behind him to gently restrain her hands. "But before you start anything that feels that good, you better tell me what time I'm supposed to have you home."

"I've got my car, remember?"

"Yeah, but I don't want you driving all that way by yourself. Especially tonight."

"You'd take me all the way out to Decatur at this hour, and then have to turn around and drive right back home?"

"I'd do anything for you." He sighed. "Including making sure your baby-sitter doesn't quit. What time is she expecting you?"

"She isn't. Not tonight."

Taking her by the shoulders, he looked into her eyes as an uneasy stirring in the pit of his stomach unsettled his well-entrenched composure. "No? Where'd you tell her you'd be spending the night?"

A smile crept across her lips. "Wouldn't be feeling just the tiniest bit possessive, would you?"

"Yeah," he admitted with an answering half smile. "And you look like you're enjoying the hell out of it."

"I am." Her eyes regained their customary twinkle as she explained. "Kris and Erin are at Elena's. She watches them for me when I need a sitter, and since she has her own family to look after, she takes the girls home with her for the night. They love the attention they get there. Elena and Manny have nine children and nearly twice as many grandchildren, and they all spoil Kris and Erin rotten, even the other kids."

"So you don't have to rush home," he murmured, his apprehension fading as quickly as it had arisen. "Unless you want to."

She said nothing as she slipped her arms around him, laying her cheek against his chest, and for a moment they remained motionless. Then, in silent agreement, they left the kitchen on their way to the bedroom.

Entering the dark room, Daniel switched on the bedside lamp before turning to Rae. The dim light heightened her quiet, golden-hued beauty, and he stared in appreciation as he took her face between his hands and gazed down into her eyes.

"Listen, Rae," he said softly, almost hesitantly. "With everything going on in your life right now, well, I don't want to make any mistakes, not about this. If it's a bad time . . ."

"It's the perfect time," she whispered.

Quickly he reached out to take her into his arms, but her arms just as quickly found him, sliding around his waist as their bodies met in perfect agreement. Need flooded through him. Desire more powerful and more basic than any he'd ever known set every nerve in his body on fire. Instinct urged him to throw her on the bed and seek immediate gratification. Only the pure, intense pleasure of holding her close, coupled with the promise of even better to come, gave him the self-control to keep from doing it.

Rae shifted restlessly against him, testing the limits of his restraint, and waves of heat engulfed them both as she pressed so tightly to him that they seemed to fuse into one. Responding to her enthusiasm, he used his hands to encourage her efforts, but she needed no prompting. Eagerly, she matched him stroke for stroke, caress for caress, touch for touch, sending new, even stronger sensations flooding through him, and when their mouths found each other, she kissed him as deeply and as hungrily as he kissed her.

Part of him wanted to linger there, enjoying the feel of her lips, her hands, but their rapidly mounting excitement wouldn't allow for such leisurely diversions. In minutes, their clothes were no more than little heaps on the floor, and he and Rae lay among the rumpled sheets on his bed, joined in the most soul-enriching experience of his life.

A host of unfamiliar emotions filled him, threatening to drown him in a sea of joy as he did his best to give her the same sense of fulfillment. When he heard her muffled cry of pleasure and felt her release, he knew he'd succeeded, and he abandoned himself to an explosion of sensations that shot through his entire body and left him feeling unexpectedly complete.

Unprepared for the sense of wholeness he'd found with Rae, he felt a pang of regret when, at last, he was forced to temporarily break the physical connection between them. It lasted only a moment, though. As she sighed in obvious satisfaction and settled into his embrace, his optimism returned full force.

For a long time they both lay still, not speaking. Words would only complicate what they'd communicated so well with their hearts, souls, and bodies. The contentment he was only beginning to know grew as he listened to Rae's rhythmic breathing. Lying beside him with her head on his chest, a leg thrown casually across his, and the fingers of one hand entwined in his chest hair, she hadn't stirred in a while. He smiled to himself. Somewhere, sometime, he must have done something incredibly good to deserve this. With an effort, he suppressed the urge to gather her even closer to him. Instead, he whispered, "Asleep?"

She rubbed her cheek against his chest as she snuggled closer to him. "Uh-uh. Enjoying."

"Me, too," he murmured, tightening his arms around her.

Looking up, she tilted her face toward him as if offering her lips for his kiss, and he didn't disappoint her. Gently he covered her mouth with his. Their urgency assuaged for the moment, they lingered over the sweet, tender exchange that said as much in its way as their earlier lovemaking had.

"Rae," he said softly, his lips poised just above hers. "Do you know how much I care for you?"

She met his gaze with wide brown eyes that sparkled with gold highlights. "Well, I . . . yes . . . if you're talking about what you said on the phone earlier."

He smiled and swallowed the lump that had formed in his throat. "Didn't think you noticed."

"I noticed," she whispered, tracing with one finger the jagged scar that the airplane crash had left on his face. "But I didn't know if you meant it."

"Well, I did." His whole body tensed, and he had to force himself not to look away while, hoping she couldn't feel the wild, erratic beating of his heart, he prepared to say words that hadn't so much as crossed his mind in years. Damn! He'd be lucky to get through this without hyperventilating or breaking into a cold sweat. "Rae." So far, so good. At least his voice hadn't cracked. "I love you with all my heart."

She didn't speak, and her expression betrayed nothing as she continued to gaze up at him. Except for the restlessness of her hand, which left his face to draw random patterns across his chest, she showed no reaction whatsoever. At last he understood the meaning of the term "deafening silence."

"Probably wouldn't be cool to ask what you think about that, would it?" He tried for a light tone but didn't quite pull it off.

Her eyes grew still wider as she ran the tip of her tongue over her lips. Inhaling deeply, she paused, then blurted, "I love you, too." The words spilled out, almost tumbling over each other, and she buried her face in the crook where his shoulder met his neck. "Why's that so frightening? We're adults, after all."

He let out a long, slow breath. "Seems like the older you get, the harder it is to put your heart on the line.

Over the years, I guess, you find out how many ways it can get broken. Gets downright scary after a while.''

She relaxed in his arms as she quietly teased, ''I always knew you had plenty of courage, but tonight you really showed your stuff. You must be the bravest man in America.''

''On this block, maybe . . . for the moment.'' Chuckling, he tightened his arms around her. ''I'm just glad I didn't pass out waiting for you to say something.''

''Sorry.'' Placing little kisses along the side of his neck, she fit her phrases in between them. ''That's not something I've had a lot of practice saying, and we haven't known each other, not really, for very long.''

''No? Feels like a lifetime to me. For the last two years, I've been stumbling around looking for something I couldn't even remember losing. Now I know what it was, but finding you only makes those two years seem even longer and emptier.'' Holding her firmly in his arms, he rolled over, turning her onto her back so he could look into her eyes. ''Maybe the words'll get easier to say when you get used to hearing them, and believe me, you're going to hear them a lot.'' Once again, he leaned down to taste the lips that could set his heart racing with no more than the slightest touch.

They made love without haste, without pressing need. Lingering over every caress, every kiss, every delightful sensation, they shared the most intimate bond possible between a man and a woman. Then, wonderfully exhausted, they lay quietly in each other's arms.

''Guess I should start thinking about going home,'' Rae finally said, sighing deeply.

''Nobody's there.''

''They'll be home early, though.'' Running a hand lightly down his neck, over his chest and stomach, and beyond, she said, ''I wouldn't want them to catch me coming home in the morning wearing the same dress I left in the night before. That's not the kind of example

I want to set for them. Besides, I've got to get to work early tomorrow.''

"Mm-hmm." Her easy caress banished all trace of fatigue and set his pulse racing yet again. "Me, too."

"I suppose if I got up really early—"

"I'll set the alarm," he said, abruptly cutting her off. Having found the woman he'd waited all his life for, he had no intention of letting go of her quite so soon.

SEVEN

In spite of rising early and racing home, Rae barely had time to run upstairs to shower before she heard Elena's car drive up.

Wrapping her wet hair in a towel, she shrugged into her thick terry-cloth robe and walked to the top of the stairway. "What's that I hear?" she called out. "Burglars in my kitchen?"

She'd made it halfway down the staircase when Kristen and Erin charged into the hall and up to meet her, shouting in unison, "Oh-la, Auntie Rae! Oh-la, Auntie Rae, kay tall?"

Ignoring their mangled Spanish, she sat down on a step and gathered them into a hug as she answered, "Missed you a whole bunch, but everything else's fine. How about you two?"

Kristen beamed. "See? I told you Auntie Rae would know what we said. She knows *everything*."

Erin gave a grudging nod but quickly perked up. "See what I got?" She waved something in front of her aunt's face with lightning speed that kept Rae from identifying the object the child plopped into her mouth

with a triumphant flourish. "Mazapan," Erin mumbled
around her mouthful.

"Candy? At this hour?" Rae gave a mock frown.
"Elena and Manny spoil you rotten."

"They were lucky to get any with my grandchildren
around," Rae's plump, motherly housekeeper said from
the bottom of the stairs. "They're too polite for my
bunch, but I saved some for them to have today. They
ate a good breakfast first, though."

"Burritos," Kris said.

"The scrambled-egg kind," Elena assured her.

"Sounds good. Thanks for taking such good care of
my girls."

"Any time," Elena replied, starting back to the
kitchen. "They're no trouble at all."

Giving the girls another squeeze, Rae said, "Today's
Friday. Know what that means?"

"Workday," they answered in unison.

"That's right." She stood up. "And I'm running a
little late, so I have to hurry and get ready. You can
keep me company if you want to, or you can play
outside for a little while."

They elected to follow her around and fill her in on
the details of their overnight visit with Elena's family
as she quickly applied her makeup, dried her hair, got
dressed, and rushed through her breakfast. When she
left, both girls ran to the porch to wave good-bye as
she backed out of the drive.

Unused to having to hurry, Rae kept an eye on the
speedometer in an attempt to curb the temptation to
make up time on the road. This morning she needed
another problem like she needed a hole in the head. An
organizer and a planner by nature, she was rarely late
for anything, and on the days she worked at the studio,
she almost always arrived ahead of the rest of the staff.
Today, Jenna had already completed the preopening
tasks by the time Rae walked into the store.

"Sorry I'm late," she said, heading for the office to deposit her purse before the workday began.

Jenna pointedly looked up at the clock. "You're not. For once, I got here early. Couldn't sleep last night."

"Something wrong?" Rae looked closely at her friend and colleague. For Jenna to have arrived early, something must be very wrong indeed.

But Jenna shook her head. "Just mad. Would you believe I've finally met a man?"

"And you're angry about it?"

"Furious. We met at childbirth class. You know what that means, don't you? He's not only married, but his wife is having a baby. And that turkey had the nerve to give me the eye. I wanted to sock him."

Rae smiled. The image of petite, blond, cuddly-looking Jenna doubling up her fist and sending it into the middle of some guy's face made her want to laugh out loud. "Maybe you misunderstood something."

"Listen, I've been around long enough to know a come-on when I see one, and that guy all but asked me out right in front of his wife. She's such a pretty girl, too. His type thinks his dark good looks, to-die-for black eyes, and Latin charm will get him anything he wants."

"Sounds to me like he made quite an impression on you."

"That's what makes me so darned mad. He's the first man in three years that I've been attracted to, and he's an eighteen-karat jerk."

"Too bad. I'm for anything that can get you here on time," Rae teased.

"Thanks a lot. See if I put in any extra hours from now on. Besides, I wanted to get here early in case *you* needed a friendly shoulder. You're usually fit to be tied after a visit with Nick and Edie. Judging from the sparkle in your eyes, though, dinner must've gone better than you expected."

"Not really," she said, her smile broadening into a grin. Not even her parents could spoil her good mood today. "After the scene I made last night, I probably won't be welcome at that restaurant for a long time."

"So what's responsible for that industrial-strength smile you're wearing? Wouldn't have anything to do with the reason Mr. Daniel MacKay's already called here three times this morning, would it?"

"Might." She couldn't help teasing her curious friend. "Did he call from home?"

"Don't know. I took his number, though." Jenna gestured at the pink call slips she'd left on Rae's desk. "All three times. He insisted."

Rae picked up one of the message forms and studied it for a moment. "Must be his work number. I'd better phone him before he gets too busy."

"I can take a hint." Jenna got up from her chair and started to leave, but in the doorway she turned around. "*He* doesn't have a pregnant wife stashed away somewhere, does he?"

Rae burst out laughing. "Of course not."

"Drop-dead gorgeous, single, and crazy about you," Jenna muttered as she walked away. "Some people have all the luck."

Still laughing, Rae reached for the telephone. Within minutes, she was speaking with Daniel.

"Just wanted to hear your voice," he said in a low, intimate tone that made her heart skip a beat. "I've missed you all morning."

She laughed softly. "It's only been a few hours."

"It's easy to see which one of us has his head in the clouds." He chuckled. "Busy?"

"Not yet. We open in about two minutes."

"I have a lot to do this morning, too. Talk to you later, sweetheart. Love you."

Before she could answer, he hung up, but the smile

his words had generated didn't stop at her lips. It made its way into her heart.

Daniel phoned several times throughout the day, and those calls, along with memories of the previous evening spent with him and thoughts of their impending dinner date, got Rae through the workday without experiencing the sinking feeling that usually accompanied fatigue. In fact, the weariness that ordinarily followed a mostly sleepless night never developed. She breezed through her work and remained wide awake even during the long drive home.

As she turned into her driveway, however, the presence of a burgundy Lexus parked in front of her home triggered a vague feeling of unease in the pit of her stomach. Although Steve often drove cars off his lot, the ones he used were Chevrolets, not expensive foreign ones like the sedan out front. Besides, it was too early for him to be picking up the girls for their weekend visit. Her anxiety increased when she entered through the back door to find the kitchen in an uncommon state of disarray. Dirty dishes filled the sink, and food in various stages of preparation sat about, apparently as Elena had left it. Throwing her purse onto a chair, Rae rushed into the hall.

"Elena?" she called over the fear-induced lump in her throat.

The living room door opened, and her housekeeper stepped out. "We're in here," she said, a serious expression in place of her usually cheerful smile.

Rae started down the hall. "Everything all right?"

Motioning for Rae to wait, Elena closed the door behind her. "Listen," she said in a low voice, "about an hour ago some people showed up asking about the little girls. They say they're your parents, and the woman looks like that picture in there, so I let them in. I didn't want to leave them alone with the kids, though. That's why the kitchen's such a mess."

Relief washed over Rae. "Thanks, you did the right thing." Impulsively, she hugged the other woman. "I'll take care of it now, and don't worry about the kitchen. Steve's picking up Kris and Erin in a little while for their weekend visit, remember? I can handle dinner for Daniel and me."

"Sure," Elena agreed, her good-natured smile returning. "But before I go, I'll get the chicken ready to put in the oven. That way you'll have plenty of time for Mr. Daniel." She headed for the kitchen without waiting for a response.

Rae turned to glare toward the living room, memories of the recent confrontation with Nick and Edie fresh in her mind as she steeled herself for this latest ordeal. If she hoped to avoid upsetting Kris and Erin, she had to find a way of dealing with her parents rationally.

Quietly, she pushed open the door and surveyed the scene. Nick leaned casually against the mantel. Edie occupied the plush wing-back chair facing away from Rae. The girls sat side by side on the sofa, listening intently to one of their grandparents' stories about Africa.

Kristen saw her first. "Auntie Rae, we've got company."

Both girls jumped up and ran over to her, pausing for hugs and kisses before launching into a barrage of questions.

"That's Missus Edie and Mr. Nick." Kristen spoke first. "Did you know that?"

Rae nodded, but the children gave her no time to speak as they continued asking questions, one after the other.

"Do we have a grandma and grandpa for real?" Erin asked.

Again Rae nodded.

"Thought so," Kristen said, frowning as if trying to make sense of it all. "She looks like my mother."

"Very much," Rae agreed.

" 'Cept old," Erin said.

Rae barely managed to stifle the laugh that rose in her throat. "Elena's getting ready to go home. Why don't you go tell her 'bye? She's in the kitchen."

Obediently, the girls trotted out of the room, and Rae closed the door, then turned to face her parents.

Edie spoke first. "Honestly, their attachment to that woman borders on unhealthy. Do you know, she wouldn't leave us alone with our own grandchildren for a second."

"Good." Rae walked over to the fireplace opposite Nick. "What did you expect Elena to do when two strangers knocked on the door and started asking about the girls? For all she knew, you could have been kidnappers."

Edie put on a haughty expression and said in her most condescending manner, "We wouldn't have had to behave in such a devious manner if you had agreed to let us see them."

"My wishes in the matter don't seem to have bothered you. You managed to get what you wanted, as always."

"Iraina, dear," Nick began.

"Call me Rae or nothing at all. Your choice. What's not your choice is when, where, or if you see the girls. That's my decision. This once, you bluffed your way in here, but believe me, it won't happen again."

"Now that they know us, how will you explain our absence from their lives?" Edie demanded.

Rae couldn't help smiling. "The same way it was always explained to me."

Nick cleared his throat. "Irai—Rae, dear, we don't want a repeat of last evening's scene. We only want to spend some time with our granddaughters."

"All right. We don't have to rehash the same old resentments, but if you want to see the girls, these are the ground rules. No overemotional scenes in their presence. No mention of your family connections—Laytons, Wyatts, or otherwise. And most important, not so much as a hint that Karen was anything less than the wonderful, loving mother they remember. Understood?''

''Of course,'' Edie responded, sounding miffed. ''Though why you continue to believe we would ever malign our own daughter is beyond me.''

The door opened, and Kristen and Erin burst into the room. ''Manny came to get Elena,'' Kris informed Rae. ''She said to tell you dinner's ready for the oven.''

''Yummy, lemon chicken,'' Erin shouted.

''You're going to Steve's this weekend, remember?'' Rae reminded her. ''In fact, I need to pack your overnight bags. Anything special you want me to put in?''

''Kermit,'' Erin yelled, jumping up and down. ''Don't forget Kermit.''

Rae laughed. ''Anything for you, Kris?''

Kristen put on her most grown-up face and shook her head. ''Nope. I don't need toys to sleep with anymore.''

''Then why don't you keep Nick and Edie company while I get your stuff together, and when Steve gets here, please let him in.''

With a warning glance at her parents, Rae left to get the children's things ready for their visit with their father.

She quickly packed all the clothes the girls would need, but it took her several minutes to locate Kermit. Pulling the stuffed toy out from under Erin's bed, she lovingly tucked it into the child's bag and started to leave with the overnight cases. At the door, however, she turned back. Smiling to herself, she picked up Petey. Kris hadn't asked for him, but somehow Rae thought the little girl might sleep better with the nondescript stuffed dog at her side. Worn smooth from years of love, the one-eyed, floppy-eared animal had sported a thick, fluffy brown coat when Karen presented him to her daughter on the child's first birthday. But even in his current condition, Kristen still preferred Petey to the newer toys strewn across her bed. Carefully, Rae wrapped him in a doll blanket and zipped him into Kris's overnight bag.

By the time she rejoined the girls and her parents, Steve had arrived. Surprised that he didn't hustle his children out the door the way he usually did when picking them up for a visit, she watched curiously as he seated himself on the sofa. With Erin on his lap and Kristen beside him, he listened as raptly as they did to Nick's stories, and soon the reason for this deviation from custom became clear. Never one to pass up an opportunity, he lavished attention on his former in-laws, taking every opportunity to present himself as the bereft husband and devoted father.

Before long, his fawning manner became tiresome, and had he not been taking her nieces with him, Rae would have welcomed his departure. Even after taking that into consideration, she wasn't altogether sorry to see him go.

"You see, dear," Edie said as they watched Steve and the girls drive off, "we managed to have a nice visit with our granddaughters without harming them. You must try to get over those irrational fears of yours."

"Yes, well, they seem to have taken it in stride, so I won't stop you from seeing them while you're in town."

Nick cleared his throat. "Actually, we can't stay as long as we'd planned to. Something has come up, and we have reservations for an early morning flight to Los Angeles. Speaking engagement. You understand how it is."

"Haven't I always?" she said dryly.

Edie rifled through her purse and pulled out a piece of paper. "Our speaking tour will keep us in the States for about a month, depending on the number of additional engagements EHS schedules for us. We've made you a copy of our itinerary as it now stands so that you can contact us if you need us for anything."

Amused, Rae took the schedule from her mother. "Thanks." Right. She certainly intended to plan her emergencies to accommodate Nick and Edie. "I imagine Elena and I can handle whatever comes up, but I'll file this anyway."

"Well, darling," Edie continued as if ticking off items on a list, "we have so much to do to get ready for our departure that we must leave you now. So lovely to see you again."

With a businesslike handshake, Rae walked her parents to the door, relieved to close it after them.

Pulling into the drive behind Rae's Blazer, Daniel watched the maroon Lexus drive away. Rae hadn't mentioned expecting company this evening, but then, she didn't have to submit her calendar for his approval. Whoa! He'd have to watch that. Possessiveness was a lousy habit to get into. It could kill even the best of relationships. All the same, he couldn't help wondering . . .

Taking the steps two at a time, he bounded onto the porch. As he raised his hand to knock, however, the door opened.

"Anxious to see me?" he teased as he walked into the house.

She nodded. Stepping wordlessly into his embrace, she hugged him tightly around the waist as she rested her head against his chest.

"Something wrong?" he asked, kissing her forehead.

"Not anymore."

"But something definitely was. Have anything to do with the car that left about the time I drove up?"

She sighed. "Nick and Edie. They came to meet the children. Fortunately, Steve got here on time for once, and the girls left with him, so they didn't stay long."

Gently, he tilted her face up so that he could look into her eyes. "Sure you're okay?"

Smiling wryly, she said, "Believe it or not, nobody said a nasty word to anybody—not overtly nasty, that is."

He smiled back at her. With his thumbs, he began a light massage along her jawline. "Well, if you could deal with all that, I guess I can handle an attack of jealousy."

Her smile deepened. "Jealous? Of what?"

"Whoever was driving that Lexus. How's a guy supposed to compete with that kind of style?"

"You don't exactly drive a junk heap yourself," she said, laughing. "Besides, what makes you think you have to compete with anyone? Or any*thing*, for that matter?"

Her words touched him somewhere so deep inside that no one else had ever come close, and the contentment they produced filled him with a gentle warmth. "Be careful, sweetheart, or you'll have me feeling so secure I'll start taking you for granted."

Stretching up on tiptoes, she reached to lock her fingers behind his neck. "Go ahead, take me for granted."

"My pleasure." He leaned down to kiss the lips that had tempted him from the moment he'd walked through the door. Beginning with a light caress that deepened ever so slowly, he took time to reacquaint himself with the pleasures of her merest touch, savoring the joy of simply being near her—until his stomach growled loudly, startling them both.

With a laugh, she said, "I'm almost afraid to ask,

considering the lousy puns you could come up with, but are you hungry?''

He grinned, all but biting his tongue to suppress the urge to make bad jokes. ''Starving. Missed lunch today. Important telephone call.''

''You should have eaten while you talked. I did.''

''But I didn't have anyone to send out for food like you did.'' His stomach rumbled again.

''We'll have dinner right away, then. Thanks to Elena, it only needs about twenty minutes in the oven. Lemon chicken.'' She led the way as they headed for the kitchen. ''We serve it with fettucini.'' She paused for a moment. ''Why is it, do you suppose, that I always seem to be feeding you pasta?''

''Your contribution to increasing my stamina?''

Laughing, she gave him a playful slap on the arm. ''Couldn't stand it, could you?''

''Oh, come on,'' he protested, capturing her hand between his. ''You begrudge me one little joke?''

''It's not the quantity,'' she teased as she freed her hand and slid the pan of chicken into the oven. ''The quality's what could use some attention.''

''Everybody's a critic.'' He reached for a cutting board to help with the salad. ''Maybe after dinner you can help me practice my puns and double entendres. Unless you have something more interesting in mind?''

''No . . . not exactly.''

Her too-casual tone immediately commanded his attention.

''I was just wondering,'' she continued, ''do you keep your pilot's license current?''

''Uh-huh,'' he answered, trying to maintain his composure while alarm bells went off in his head.

''Would it cover small private planes as well as commercial airliners?''

''It would.''

''Have you ever flown one of those?''

"Lots of times, but not recently."

"But you could if you wanted to?"

"I could." He placed the tomato he had cut up into the salad bowl, pushed aside the knife and the cutting board, and studied her expression while trying to figure out where her questions were taking them. "What's on your mind?"

Seemingly oblivious to his curious stare, she went on tearing lettuce into bite-sized pieces as she asked, "How difficult would it be to rent a plane like that?"

"With the right credentials and the right price? No problem." He reached over and took the lettuce from her. Then, grasping her shoulders, he turned her to face him. "And that, my friend, was your last free answer. Let's cut to the chase. What exactly do you want to know?"

Her eyes widened, but otherwise her expression remained calm. Too calm. Somehow he felt as though she had shut herself away from him when she said, "I've never been up in a small plane, that's all. It must be different from riding in passenger jets."

"You're right about that." He continued to gaze into her inscrutable eyes. Though they told him nothing, the direction in which she'd steered the discussion suggested one highly unlikely explanation. "Rae, do you want me to take you flying?"

"Yes," she said slowly, as if searching for exactly the right words. "We don't have plans for this evening . . ."

"Tonight? Are you serious?" For a moment, he felt as if the world had stopped spinning, sending him into a free-fall through space.

"Yes." Her voice softened, but her strange, detached demeanor didn't change.

"Are you sure? Absolutely sure?"

She nodded. "But if you don't want to, that's okay."

"It's not that." Then what the hell was it? The last thing he wanted to do tonight, or at any other time, was to take her up in a plane, so why couldn't he just tell her that? "If you want to go flying, we will, but we'd have to find some place to rent an airplane."

"The airport's about ten minutes from here, over on Farm Road Seven-thirty, the road we took to Black Creek Lake."

"Yeah, I know the one."

"I've seen signs for rental planes there."

Their whole conversation had taken on an unreal quality, and again he studied her face for some clue to the motive for her peculiar request. Search as hard as he might, however, her eyes betrayed nothing.

With a shrug of resignation, he said, "We'd better find out what's available and if somebody'll be there to handle the rental."

"I can call and ask."

"I'll do it." Turning, he headed for the hall.

"Phone book's in the drawer of the telephone stand," she called to him.

Still baffled by Rae's sudden suggestion, he dialed the number listed for the aircraft rental service. With any luck, nobody would answer.

What could have possessed her to ask him to take her flying? And what had made him agree to do it? Considering what had happened the last time she'd flown in an airplane he'd piloted, he couldn't imagine her ever trusting him in that capacity again.

He heard a click, and a strange voice said, "Hello?"

So much for relying on luck. Briefly, he explained what he wanted, and after making preliminary arrangements for hiring the plane, he returned to the kitchen in time to see Rae set a platter full of pasta topped by delicious-looking chicken in the middle of the table.

"What did you find out?" she asked from a distance he didn't know how to bridge.

"All set." He sat down in the chair she indicated.

Placing the salad bowl beside the chicken dish, she joined him at the table. "Good."

Although he tried, he couldn't keep up his end of the conversation during dinner as his mind continually drifted to the upcoming flight. How would Rae react to finding herself in a real aircraft with him at the controls? If she panicked after takeoff, it would be a while before he could set down. Had she taken that into consideration?

Fortunately, she didn't seem to notice his preoccupation. Nor did she appear to be aware of how little he ate. Without even trying, she'd found the perfect appetite suppressant for him.

As soon as they finished, they tidied the kitchen, and while Rae changed her clothes, he waited on the porch. Instead of bracing him for the coming ordeal, though, the hot, muggy air felt anything but refreshing. By the time she joined him, dressed in jeans and a sleeveless top, he had almost decided to call the whole thing off. Only her purposeful manner kept him from canceling the flight. Disregarding the uneasiness that had settled in his gut, he pulled his car around to the front of the house and waited for her to get in on the passenger's side, then headed in the direction of the airport.

He glanced at her as he turned onto the highway. In a few minutes, they would be airborne. What would he see in her eyes then?

EIGHT

Rae paced back and forth across the small office while she waited for Daniel to finish filling out the required forms for renting the airplane.

Glancing over at him, she wondered if he'd noticed her nervousness. She'd tried hard to hide it, and she'd watched for signs that he might have picked up on her anxiety. So far, she had detected none. Throughout their discussion of the venture, he had seemed totally at ease, except that he hadn't eaten much even after claiming to be famished. But then, neither had she. The oppressive heat was probably to blame for that. Nothing could kill an appetite faster than temperatures in the hundreds.

Daniel looked up from the completed paperwork. Motioning for her to accompany him, he held the door for her as they left the cramped little office.

Rae lengthened her stride to match his as they set off to find the craft that they would use. "I can't believe we're really doing this," she said softly.

He stopped in his tracks. "Second thoughts?"

"Not at all."

For the first time, she perceived in him an undercur-

123

rent of apprehension. Had he sensed her fear and re-
acted to it, or was it something else? When she had
first mentioned flying, he'd looked surprised. After that,
however, he'd seemed comfortable with her suggestion,
and she had turned her attention inward, focusing all
her energy on keeping her edginess from showing. She
could well have missed any subtle signals that might
have indicated a lack of enthusiasm on his part. In her
attempt to exorcise her own ghosts, had she left him
struggling with his?

Giving him one last chance to back out, she said,
"With all the time you spend in simulators, though,
you're probably bored stiff by the thought of climbing
into another cockpit. We don't have to do this, if you'd
rather not."

"It's okay with me either way." He took her by the
shoulders, turning her to face him as he stared hard
into her eyes. "But if you have any doubt about it,
now's the time to say so."

She shook her head. "No doubts," she lied, hoping
her features wouldn't betray the deception.

Apparently satisfied with her answer, he slipped an
arm around her, and they continued directly to the plane
they had rented. White with black-and-gold stripes, the
sleek-looking little aircraft appeared to be well main-
tained. Daniel, however, left nothing to chance. In spite
of the rental agent's assurance that the plane had been
fueled and readied for them, he walked slowly around
it, shining a large, bright flashlight over every inch of
its body. Occasionally he squatted for a closer look at
some part of its underside as he carefully checked each
detail, until finally, the inspection completed to his satisfaction, he called to her.

Rae's stomach lurched, and she fought the urge to
run away. Instead, she forced herself to climb into the
seat he designated, her anxiety mounting as she watched
him walk around and get in beside her. When they both

had buckled themselves securely into the little aircraft, he looked over at her.

"Ready?" he asked in a quiet, serious-sounding voice, examining her as intently as he had the plane.

Unable to speak through her clenched teeth, she nodded.

"Then here we go." Putting on his headset, he reached for the controls.

Unlike the simulator she had operated, the rental plane had only one engine, yet the uneasiness that rushed through her as it roared to life far exceeded the tension she'd felt before. This time the sights, sounds, and movement were real. As the plane, under Daniel's control, began slowly taxiing to the runway, she gripped the edges of her seat and leaned forward. The ordeal she had avoided for two years was under way, and she barely had time to get used to the relatively leisurely ground speed before they began accelerating toward takeoff, a rougher event than she had expected because their small plane registered the imperfections of the runway considerably more than a larger craft would have. Then they lifted off.

Immediately, the ride smoothed out. Concentrating on maintaining her self-control, she refused to look up as they climbed higher and higher until she felt a strange separation from the earth, the likes of which she had never before experienced.

When at last they leveled off, Daniel turned to her. "You okay?"

She nodded.

"Then where to?"

"Anywhere." Tearing her gaze away from the red switch she'd focused on to keep her eyes from straying to the window, she glanced over at him. "Doesn't matter."

"West, then, so we don't get tangled up in the traffic

at Dallas-Forth Worth airport. Want to see your home first?"

"I . . . I guess so."

He made a turn that left butterflies in her stomach as she felt the motion of the aircraft much more distinctly than that of an airliner.

"There," he said. "Just ahead."

"Where?" Forcing herself to look out the window, she stared in the direction he indicated, but she could see nothing except the groups of lights that marked the surrounding towns. As hard as she tried, she couldn't distinguish her home from the others rushing by below them. "I don't see it."

"We'll go back."

She met with the same lack of success on their second pass, and when he offered to try once more, she declined.

"I'd only miss it again."

He nodded. Continuing on a course of his choosing, he spoke little throughout the remainder of their flight except to point out the various landmarks they passed over. She missed most of them. Only Lake Bridgeport, a body of water large enough to recognize even in the dark, looked familiar to her, and it was while studying its dark, shiny surface that she realized that her fear had been replaced by curiosity. Little by little, she relaxed, eventually becoming comfortable with the motion of the small plane until she actually began to enjoy the experience. Only when they began to descend did her alarm return.

"Are we landing?" she asked, her voice betraying her distress.

"In about five more minutes," he replied, using the same calm, soothing tone he'd used the first time they'd spoken. "It's okay, Rae. We're almost home."

Her irrational fear was no longer her secret. In her panic, she'd given herself away, but he made no mention of it. Transfixed, she stared out the window the way she had done once before, watching the ground rise up to meet them.

Setting the plane gently on the ground, Daniel slowed almost to a stop before taxiing back to the apron where their trip had begun, and as they rolled to a standstill, he wasted no time shutting the engine down. Without a word, he opened his door and climbed out, leaving her alone to regain her composure.

Rae drew a deep, steadying breath, waiting for the rubbery sensation in her legs to subside. She'd done it! She'd faced head-on the thing she most feared, and she'd survived. She had even enjoyed it to an extent. Only the landing had threatened to unnerve her, and in the end, she'd got through that, too. Slowly, the sick feeling in the pit of her stomach went away, and as she got out of the plane, a strange euphoria took over.

"Wait up," she called, running to catch up with Daniel, who was strolling slowly toward the office.

Though he reached for her hand, he didn't say a word, looking straight ahead as he proceeded to the office to settle with the rental agent. After he had finished taking care of the details, he headed silently for his car.

"That was great," she said, settling comfortably into the passenger's seat.

A strange expression crossed his face as he glanced at her. "Was it?"

"Didn't you think so?"

With a shrug, he started the engine, retreating into silence once more.

Rae filled the conversational void without his assistance, her usual reticence nowhere in evidence. On an adrenaline high after conquering her greatest fear, she couldn't stop the continuous stream of triviality spilling from her mouth. She was still babbling at the verbal equivalent of a sprinter's pace when they arrived at her house.

Daniel parked on the street, and with hardly a pause in her monologue, Rae reached for the door handle. She was halfway out of the car before she realized that he remained motionless, his hands resting on the steering wheel as he stared straight ahead.

Looking back over her shoulder, she asked, "You're coming in, aren't you?"

He turned to stare at her, an odd expression on his face. "Yeah," he finally said, opening his door to get out.

She waited for him to walk around the car to join her, taking his hand as they proceeded up the walk together. "Thanks for tonight, Daniel."

She started up the first step, but he stopped her. Firmly grasping her arm, he turned her to face him.

Fixing her with a look that seemed capable of penetrating to her very soul, he asked, "That mean I passed the test?"

Immediately her exhilaration evaporated, leaving her feeling empty. "That's what you thought it was?"

After another long, hard look at her, he abruptly sat down on the top step, resting his elbows on his knees and staring into the distance. "Yeah, it occurred to me."

"What kind of test?" she asked, sinking down to sit beside him. "Courage? Strength? Willpower? I've already seen all that. What else would I want you to prove?"

"Competence, maybe?" He gave a short, humorless laugh. "After what happened the last time you rode in a plane I piloted, maybe you wanted to see how it would feel to find yourself in that position again. Maybe some part of you still wonders what I did wrong."

She inhaled sharply, his words hitting her like a

physical blow. "But you know how I feel about that . . . don't you?"

"I know what you've told me," he said, studying his hands as if they held all the secrets of the universe. "Sometimes, though, what you say and what you feel aren't the same thing."

"I see," she said, tears filling her eyes. "It comes down to trust, and you think I'm a liar."

"God, no!" In a single motion, he reached to take her in his arms. "That's not what I meant, Rae. It's just that last night we had something so good. Hell, I thought that only happened in the movies. Then, this evening, everything changed. Something was going on with you. Something important. But you shut me out of it, and it scared me to death. I don't want you to be able to push me out of your life whenever you feel like it. I want to be more important to you than that."

"You are," she whispered, holding tightly to him as she buried her face in his shoulder. "It's only because of that, because I trust you so much, that I asked you to take me flying tonight. Daniel, I wasn't testing you. It was *me*.

"Until tonight, I hadn't been near an airplane since the . . . the accident. Watching one fly overhead was enough to make me feel sick. Actually getting into one was out of the question. That's been a problem. You know . . . with the New Orleans store. I haven't been back there since the opening two years ago, and even though Jenna's made a few trips for me, it's not the same as giving it my personal attention. Lately, I've felt the pressure more and more. It's only been in the past couple of weeks, though, that I started to think it might be possible for me to get over my fear . . . only since I've known you. I haven't forgotten what happened that day, how you did everything possible to bring us home. And I knew if I had any chance of getting past that paralyzing terror, it would only be with you. I could never trust anyone else enough for that. I know I should have been straight with you about this from the beginning. I'm sorry."

"No," he murmured, the edge of bitterness gone from his voice. "You're not responsible for my insecurities." He leaned back against the porch railing, keeping his arms loosely around her. "It's just that I feel like I've had to defend every single thing I've done since that plane went down. The minute I woke up after surgery, the questions started—most of them about my competence—and they've never stopped. The NTSB ruling didn't even slow them down. Pilots still resent me scoring their check rides. Other instructors don't like having me at the flight academy. They act like they're afraid the taint might rub off on them. Even some flight attendants have told me they're glad I'm not flying anymore. Guess a part of me wondered whether you doubted me, too."

"I'd never have had the guts to get in that plane with anybody but you." Leaning away from him, she looked directly into his eyes. "Flying won't ever be easy for me, but because of you, it'll never be as hard again, either. And you know, for a little while I even enjoyed it. I think the girls would, too."

"You'd allow that?"

She nodded. "With you."

She caught a glimmer of emotion in his eyes just before he looked away from her, but the huskiness shading his voice was harder to hide as he said, "You'll never know how much that means to me."

"Enough to forgive me for not being up-front with you about my hang-ups?" she asked as she settled back into his embrace.

"Sure," he murmured. "But why didn't you tell me about it earlier?"

"Guess I was afraid you wouldn't go through with it if you knew." She paused, looking up to study his features. "Would you have taken me up if you'd known how scared I was?"

"Don't know." He sighed. "No. Probably not."

"Well, then I'm glad you didn't know. Tonight was a major victory for me. Now I think I'll finally be able to come to terms with my phobia about airplanes." She paused briefly while she gathered her thoughts. "Something else happened, too, Daniel, something I hadn't counted on. I got a chance to show you how much I believe in you."

"Then it was worth it," he said, brushing her forehead with a kiss.

"Would I be pushing it too far to ask you another favor?"

"You got it," he answered without hesitation.

She smiled up at him, her feelings for him strengthened by his readiness to respond to her needs. "When the time comes for me to make that trip to New Orleans, will you come along and hold my hand?"

"You know I will." One corner of his mouth lifted in a half smile, and his eyes twinkled suggestively as he gazed down at her. "But first I need a favor from you."

Eager to take him up on his unspoken proposition, she replied as quickly to his request as he had to hers. "Name it."

"Warm up that lemon chicken?"

Rae burst out laughing as she pushed herself away from him and stood up. "So much for romance."

"Romance is hard work on an empty stomach." Taking the hand she offered, he pulled himself to his feet. "Feed me, and see how romantic I can get."

"Promises, promises," she teased as they went inside and headed straight for the kitchen. It took only minutes to heat the lemon chicken and not much longer for them to down every bite. When they finished, Daniel began loading their dishes into the dishwasher as he casually asked, "How do you feel about overnight guests?"

Rae continued wiping the countertop, trying to suppress the grin that threatened to spread itself all over her face. "Depends. I usually decide on a case-by-case basis."

Without so much as a smile, he turned back to the dishwasher, placing the last glass in the rack. "That's not funny," he said flatly.

Drying her hands, she walked up behind him and hugged him as she laid her cheek against the soft cotton shirt covering his back. "I was teasing. Guess I didn't pick a very funny subject."

"Guess you didn't." He turned around, drawing her close as, with one hand, he tilted her face toward his. "I love you, Rae. I can't joke about sharing you with other men."

"It's been so long since I've had 'other men' in my life that I've forgotten how unfunny jokes like that can be. Sorry."

"Maybe you can make it up to me," he said, giving her his breathtaking half smile.

"Maybe so," she answered, her pulse quickening as she contemplated the methods she intended to use to achieve that goal. "We've got the rest of the night to work on it. Even longer. The girls won't be home until Sunday morning."

His eyes reflected his willingness to help her succeed, and he kissed her gently before they left the kitchen together to walk, arm in arm, upstairs to her bedroom. When they entered, however, Daniel paused in the doorway, leaning against the doorjamb as he gazed at the portrait of Rae that hung over her bed. For a few minutes, he studied it intently while, intrigued, she watched his expression change again and again. Slowly he shifted his attention from the picture back to her, examining her features with the same concentration he had given her likeness until, at last, he drew her into his warm embrace.

"Beautiful," he murmured.

"You're biased," she said with a little laugh.

"Could be." Holding her close, he glanced back up at the portrait. "But it takes my breath away. It's even better than the photo it was painted from. Wish I had it hanging in my bedroom."

"Take it."

"You can't just give it away like that."

Impatient to begin making up for her earlier transgression, she shifted in his arms, loosening his embrace enough to enable her to reach his shirt buttons. As she began unfastening them, she said, "Why not? It's mine."

He inhaled sharply at her touch. "Yeah, but that's a pretty valuable present to be giving away to just anybody."

"In the first place," she began as she lightly stroked his chest where his shirt hung open, "you're not just anybody. And second, I could use some help with this apology thing. I'm gonna do it right, whether you like it or not."

Without warning, he swept her off her feet and carried her to the bed, laying her gently on it as he positioned himself above her. Gazing down at her, he smiled. "What d'ya wanna bet I like it?"

With a laugh, Rae reached up to grab each side of his unbuttoned shirt, and tugging firmly, she pulled him down to her. Beginning slowly, she gradually took him from tender warmth to fiery passion as she used everything at her disposal to make him forget she'd ever had anything to apologize for. Then they fell asleep in each other's arms.

NINE

Daniel's arm landed hard on Rae's stomach, startling her awake; then as quickly as it had dropped across her, it was gone again as Daniel thrashed around in bed.

"No!" he yelled, sitting bolt upright. "Damn!"

Quickly, she sat up beside him. Taking him by both arms, she shook him gently. "Daniel?" she said, keeping her tone soft but firm.

For a moment he seemed disoriented, but as realization began to dawn in his eyes, he pulled her into a tight hug. "Damn," he muttered.

Acting on instinct, she wrapped her arms securely around him. She could feel his heart hammering in his chest, and the clamminess of his skin explained the shiver that vibrated through his body as he clung to her. Gently, she began to stroke his hair as she murmured, "It's okay. It's over now. Everything's all right." She knew the words didn't matter. Only the familiarity of the voice saying them and the nearness of someone he trusted would help dispel the confusion left over from a horrifying nightmare, and she used a soothing tone as she repeated the phrases like a mantra.

At first, her efforts had little effect. Eventually, however, the tension began to ease from his body. Still, he didn't release her, though he relaxed his hold a little.

"Damn," he muttered again.

"That happen often?" she asked softly as she continued her comforting caresses.

"Every night at first, but not for a long time."

"Not until I dredged up all those bad memories."

"Forget it. I got more out of that flight than you did, and I wouldn't trade it for ten nightmares."

"You might get the chance to pay up," she said ruefully. "This may not be the last of them."

"Same one—every time." He drew her across his lap and buried his face in her shoulder. "God, I wish I could make that damn plane fly."

"I know. I've had it, too, or something like it, and every time, I wake up feeling like I missed another chance to change what happened. But that's just a pipe dream. All we can do now is find a way to live with it. Guess you'd have a better chance of that if I hadn't brought it up again."

"Not your fault I have bad dreams, sweetheart," he murmured. "And if there's any chance of stopping them, it'll be because of you."

Tears stung her eyes, but she fought against them. They'd had enough gloom for one night. Trying to lighten the mood, she said, "Let's start by swearing off lemon chicken right before bedtime."

He almost smiled as he smoothed her hair away from her face. Placing his hands behind her head, he lifted her toward him to take her mouth in a long, leisurely kiss.

"I love you, Rae," he whispered, his lips moving lightly against hers as he spoke. "I have since the first time I heard your voice, and some part of me knew I wouldn't find peace until we were together again."

"Me, too." Reaching up, she touched his lips

lightly, tracing them with one finger. "A grief counselor tried to tell me it was like hostage syndrome, but I knew that wasn't it. What happened with us was, well, weird. Sometimes I'd find myself listening to every conversation within earshot for something I wasn't even sure I'd recognize. It happened everywhere, in parking lots, grocery stores, the post office, everywhere."

He nodded. "Restaurants were the worst. I'd catch myself concentrating so hard on hearing other people's conversations that I didn't know what the person with me was saying."

"Is that so?" Glad for a chance to break the last link to the nightmare's depressing spell, she grinned and turned to place her hands on his shoulders. Pressing him back against the sheets, she used her body to hold him still. "And what about all those quiet dinners you ate alone at home?"

He chuckled. "I had plenty of those." Suddenly, he grabbed her hands and tugged, bringing her full weight against him before he rolled over, reversing their positions. "Besides, if I'd been with the right person, I wouldn't have been listening to everybody else, would I?"

"Maybe not," she admitted, not bothering to struggle against her gentle captivity. "Anyway, it doesn't matter anymore. We found each other."

His mouth came down hard over hers. Firm and demanding, his tongue entered like silken fire to steal her breath away. Hungrily, she kissed him back. Desire coursed through her body as she encouraged his hot, probing caress, using her lips, tongue, teeth—everything at her disposal—to answer his welcome invasion.

Her position, however, limited her response. Pinned to the bed under his weight, she could only accept pleasure as he slid his hands over her bare shoulders. Moving down, his hands found the sides of her breasts, pressed flat against his chest, and without taking his lips from hers, he transferred his weight to one elbow to allow his other hand room to explore. Softly he stroked the already taut nipple.

Someone moaned, but the sound was lost in their throats, and Rae couldn't be sure whom it came from. She didn't care. Nothing mattered but the throbbing excitement he sent surging through her body, and when he shifted to allow her more freedom of movement, she strained toward him.

Abruptly, his lips abandoned hers. For a moment she felt a twinge at their loss, but then they turned up again, replacing his hand at her breast. With the same skill and thoroughness he had used to ravish her mouth, he now urged her to even greater heights of physical enjoyment, and just when she thought his single-minded attention would drive her mad, his lips began to move again. Traveling downward, he teased at her navel before continuing lower.

Wave after wave of pleasure washed over her, each one more intense than the last, until a final thrilling burst erupted deep inside her. Gasping, she surrendered to the sensations spreading throughout her body, unable to think of anything else until they began to subside.

Ever so slowly, she returned to awareness to find herself cradled in Daniel's warm embrace, and she drowsily nestled into his arms.

"Sweet dreams," he whispered, gently kissing her tender lips.

"But you," she started to object, "what about . . ."

"It's okay, sweetheart. We have all weekend."

"Mm-hmm." Safe in the warmth of his encircling arms, she drifted back to sleep.

Loud, rhythmic pounding jarred Rae awake. Instantly alert, she leapt out of bed to find Daniel sitting up and reaching for his jeans.

"Somebody at the front door," he said in answer to her unasked question.

Grabbing her robe, she quickly pulled it on as she asked, "What time is it?"

"Not quite seven-thirty."

"Who could it be at this hour?" She belted her robe securely around her waist, crossed to the window, and lifted the curtain aside. Steve's car was parked at the curb behind Daniel's.

"Oh, no," she gasped. "Steve brought the girls home a day early."

Walking up behind her, Daniel grasped her shoulders firmly. "It's okay. They've already seen my car, but they don't know when I got here. Go on down and let them in. Maybe they won't ask any questions." He leaned over to give her a quick kiss on the cheek.

As he stepped back out of view, she opened the window and called out, "Are the girls okay?"

Both children and their father appeared on the front walk from the direction of the porch. Looking up at her, they gave synchronized nods.

"I'm on my way down."

By the time she had shut the window and closed the curtains, Daniel had vanished.

Expecting at every turn to run into him, she hurried down the stairs to the foyer, but as she approached the front door, he still hadn't appeared. With a last glance around, she let Steve and the children in.

"About time," Steve muttered as he set the girls' bags inside. "What took you so long?"

Bending down to give her nieces welcome-home kisses, she answered irritably, "I was upstairs, and you know it." Concerned about the unexpected change of plans, she turned her attention to the girls. "I didn't expect you home today. Anything wrong?"

"Nah," Steve answered for them, his voice full of self-righteous indignation. "They started whining to come home, so I brought 'em. You got a problem with that?''

She bit her lip to keep from snapping at Steve in front of his daughters. "Certainly not.''

"I'm hungry,'' Erin complained in a whiny voice that added credence to Steve's explanation.

"You haven't had breakfast?'' she asked, glaring at Steve, though she spoke to the girls.

Looking at the floor, Kristen shook her head.

"Then let's go get something to eat. Your dad knows the way out.''

She ushered the children to the kitchen, and although her invitation pointedly excluded Steve, he followed them anyway. As they filed into the cozy room, nobody could have been more surprised than she to find Daniel standing at the counter calmly stirring a bowl of batter.

He smiled as if nothing were out of the ordinary. "Looks like we're gonna need more pancakes.''

"Well, yes, I guess so. You must've heard the commotion at the front door.'' She hoped her voice betrayed nothing of her agitation.

"Yeah.'' He cracked an egg into the bowl. "Ham's in the microwave thawing. Forgot to ask where you keep the griddle, though.''

Walking past him, she removed the appliance from the cabinet and handed it to him. "Plug it in over there,'' she said, pointing toward the outlet.

"Well, well, well,'' Steve drawled as Daniel turned his back to plug in the electric griddle. "What've we got here? Saint Daniel fall off his pedestal?''

Whirling back around to face Steve, Daniel radiated more steam than the heating griddle, and, alarmed, Rae stepped in front of him.

"Actually, I'm the saint. Daniel's the hero, remember?'' she said, surprising herself with her calm-sounding, if somewhat sarcastic, reply. "Not that it's any of your business, but I invited him for breakfast this morning.''

"And dinner last night, I'll bet." Steve smirked.

"I'm hungry!" Erin complained insistently, demanding attention.

Lifting an eyebrow, Rae frowned at her brother-in-law, hoping the silent warning would be enough to make him drop the subject. "Excuse us, Steve, I have to get the girls washed up. Just let yourself out."

"Yeah, I get it," he responded as he started to leave. In the doorway, however, he turned back around and sneered, "I get it, all right. From now on, you two better be careful around my kids."

Afraid of losing control of her temper, Rae refrained from replying as she stared in frustration at his retreating back. One glance at Daniel told her that he, too, felt like throttling Steve. Like her, though, he managed to withhold comment.

Dampening some paper towels, Rae set about washing her nieces' faces and hands while Daniel poured pancake batter onto the heated griddle. But the routine tasks and their efforts at cheerful conversation couldn't restore the normally pleasant atmosphere of the homey kitchen, and both girls remained glum.

"Don't want milk," Erin whined as Rae set the child's glass down beside her plate of pancakes and ham. "Want a soda."

"You know you can't have soda for breakfast," Rae said firmly.

"Cookie does." Pouting, Erin nudged the glass of milk as far away from her as possible without pushing it off the table. "Cookie only drinks soda."

Rae put Erin's milk back beside her plate. "I don't care what Cookie does."

Giving her aunt a defiant look, Erin challenged her not to care how Steve's girlfriend acted. "Well, she made Krissy cry."

Rae looked over at Kristen. So that explained the child's mood as she sat absolutely still, staring at her untouched pancakes. Reaching over to stroke her niece's cheek gently, she asked, "Want to tell me about it?"

Tears began to slide down Kris's face as she shook her head, but Erin quickly jumped in to explain. "Cookie threw Petey away."

"Oh, no," Rae said as Kristen burst into heart-breaking sobs. Pushing her breakfast out of her way, she gathered the little girl into her lap, cuddling her comfortingly while blinking back tears of her own.

"Who's Petey?" Daniel asked quietly.

"A stuffed dog," Rae said. "A gift from Karen."

"That's a shame." With a thoughtful look, Daniel patted Kristen's hair. "Today's Saturday, though. No garbage pickup. We could go over there and try to find him."

Rae gave him a grateful smile. How could anyone not love a man who would willingly spend his weekend sorting through garbage for a broken-hearted child's stuffed toy?

Before she could speak, however, Erin chimed in. "I got him back already, didn't I, Krissy?"

Somewhat calmer, the older child nodded.

"Last night," Erin went on, "after Daddy and Cookie went to bed, I sneaked in the kitchen and got Petey out of the trash can. Only I dumped it over, and then I got caught. But I didn't let 'em get Petey away from me again."

"They yelled at Eri, but she wouldn't give 'em Petey," Kristen confirmed, sniffling. "Not even when Cookie spanked her."

"That woman spanked Erin?" Furious at Steve for failing to protect his children, as well as for his hypocritical comments about her relationship with Daniel, Rae had to struggle to maintain control.

Nodding, Erin said, "But Daddy made her stop 'cuz

he said you'd get mad." She broke into a mischievous grin. "Did you get mad, Auntie Rae?"

Rae ignored the goading comment, and as her temperature returned to normal, she grinned at her spirited, red-haired niece. "I'm glad you got Petey back."

"He's all dirty and smelly," Kristen said softly.

"We've washed him before," Rae reminded her. "Don't worry. We'll get him so clean and sweet-smelling he won't even remember being thrown away."

Her composure restored, Kristen slipped off Rae's lap and climbed back into her own chair. Gazing across the table at Daniel, she took a big bite of her cold pancakes, washing it down with milk before she asked in her usual, much-too-grown-up manner, "Mr. Daniel, did you kill my mother?"

TEN

Stunned, Daniel stared at the wide-eyed child. How could he answer her question without destroying any chance whatsoever of earning the love and respect of the children he had begun to hope he would one day help raise? How much of what had gone on in the cockpit that day would a five-year-old understand? And what about Erin? Could a three-year-old even begin to comprehend what had prompted him to make those critical decisions? Would they blame him for not making the right ones? What responsibility would he bear in their hearts and minds for not recognizing that a mechanical malfunction had sent him the wrong signals? Had he killed their mother? Yes.

Alarm flashed in Rae's eyes, but it wasn't reflected in her voice as she asked, "Where would you get an idea like that, Kris?"

"Daddy told us," Kristen answered, taking another drink of milk.

Outwardly less concerned over this matter than she had been about the damage to her stuffed dog, the child continued her breakfast, but how closely associated the

145

two losses had become in her mind was anybody's guess. To her, that toy might represent her mother.

"Well, baby, Steve was wrong." Rae leaned forward, placing herself protectively between Daniel and her niece. "Daniel wouldn't harm anyone."

Kristen nodded. "That's what I told Daddy, but he said Mr. Daniel was driving the plane when Mommy died."

"Can you drive a airplane, Dan-yul?" Erin chimed in, spreading syrup across her face as she tried to wipe her mouth clean.

"Yes," he said, recovering from the shock that had kept him silent.

Erin bounced excitedly in her seat. "Take me in a airplane, Dan-yul. Take me in a airplane."

Rae picked up the energetic little girl. "First things first, and right now, you and I need to get cleaned up." She gave Daniel an encouraging smile. "Be right back. Coming, Kris?"

"Nope." Kristen pushed her empty plate away from her, refusing to accept the change of subject. "I want to talk to Mr. Daniel some more."

Already on her way out of the room, Rae came to an abrupt halt. When she started back toward them, however, he motioned her away.

"Kristen's right." Rising, he started clearing the table. "We need to talk."

As Rae, with Erin in tow, disappeared through the door and up the stairs, he forced himself to swallow the words he knew would bring her back to his side. This he must do without her help. Any hope he had of retaining even a small portion of the trust that had begun to build between him and Rae's nieces depended on how they accepted his account of the events that had taken their mother's life. He owed them nothing less than the truth.

In silence, Kristen helped him clear the table, and

when the last sticky drop of syrup had been wiped away, they reseated themselves in the same chairs they had occupied at breakfast.

Yet again, he found himself alone, preparing to defend the actions he had taken in the moments before the crash—a position he was all too familiar with. He had been interviewed countless times by New World officials and NTSB investigators; he had become the lone focus of many a news media inquisition; he had given testimony at a public hearing, facing a crowd that included many who had lost family members in the accident. Compared to explaining to Kristen how her mother died, all that had been a cakewalk.

Forcing himself to broach the subject, he said softly, "Kris, Steve told you the truth. I was the pilot that day."

She nodded. "Thought so."

"Want me to tell you about it?"

Fixing her wide-eyed, innocent gaze on him, she said, "Yes, please."

"Okay." He drew a deep breath. "Why don't you tell me what you already know about it? Then I'll know where to start."

With a sigh, Kristen propped her elbows on the table, resting her chin in her hands as a frown puckered her little face. "Well, Mommy went to New Orleans to have a party for the new store. On the way back, she was in a plane crash and the door was closed and she died."

"Okay," he said, clearing his throat in an attempt to move the lump that had formed there. "You see, an airplane has special doors for people to use when there's an emergency."

"When something bad happens?"

"That's right. Something real bad happened that day, and we crashed."

"Auntie Rae said the plane broke."

"Two things broke." He paused, trying to decide how to explain a faulty emergency light to a very young but very bright little girl. "First, one of the engines stopped working."

Her frown deepened as she puzzled over the idea. "How many motors does a plane have?"

"The one I flew had two of them, one under each wing."

"Wing motors?"

He couldn't help smiling at the child's confusion. "I'll show you if you'll get me a piece of paper and a pencil."

"In my desk, Kris," Rae said from the doorway.

Wearing no makeup and dressed in jeans, an oversized T-shirt, and tennis shoes, she looked more like one of the children than their guardian as she walked over to him. When both girls ran off to find the supplies he'd requested, he stood up, pulling her into his arms as he leaned against the table. He had no idea how long she had been listening. He only knew that her presence made the ordeal easier to bear as she returned his embrace. Slipping her arms around his waist, she began to massage away the pain that was knifing its way through his lower back, and by the time the children returned, it had diminished to no more than a twinge.

"Couldn't find a pencil," Kristen said as she handed him a piece of typing paper and a fat green crayon.

"That's all right," he answered, releasing Rae as he placed Kristen's chair beside his so that she would be able to see better. "The way I draw, it won't matter at all."

When he sat down and picked up the crayon, both children climbed into the chair next to him, and Rae, half sitting on the edge of the table, remained at his side as he began to sketch. Soon he'd completed a rough copy of an airplane, more or less from the side. Adding the engine, he explained, "There's one on the other side, too, but none up front like in a car."

The girls studied the picture while he went on. "Most of the time a pilot uses both engines, but if one quits working, he can fly the plane just fine with only the other one."

"Like what happened to your plane?" Kristen asked quietly.

"That's right. A pilot knows right away when something goes wrong with an engine, but because he's way up front, he can't see which one is broken. He has a light that comes on to tell him which one to turn off. In my plane, the wrong light came on."

He paused as he attempted to gauge the effect of his words on the two little girls. Remaining uncharacteristically quiet, Erin seemed not to be listening. Kristen, however, focused on his drawing as if she expected it to yield the answers she sought, and as he watched, realization lit up her features.

"Oh!" Her wide eyes grew even larger as she whispered, "You turned off the wrong motor."

He nodded, trying not to flinch when she looked up at him. "And we crashed."

"You and Auntie Rae didn't die."

"No, we didn't," he said, stifling the urge to apologize for being alive.

As much to keep from having to meet Kristen's searching gaze as to help her understand, he turned the sheet of paper over and began sketching an overview of the interior of an airplane. However, he could feel her eyes trained on him, threatening his composure.

"Passengers sit along here." He added the appropriate markings along both sides of his crude reproduction. "Way up here is where the pilot sits."

"Where you were?"

"Uh-huh. Rae and your mother sat right about here." He marked their approximate location, glancing at Rae for confirmation. She nodded and he continued, highlighting the relevant spots on the sketch as he spoke. "This plane has emergency doors up front and in the rear, but the ones we'll be talking about right now are the ones in the middle over the wings—especially the one closest to where Karen was sitting."

Kristen pointed to one of the heavy green marks that represented emergency exits. "This one?"

"Yes." He stared hard at the dark emerald symbol, almost willing it to open, even now, and release the eleven souls that had been trapped behind it. If he found himself wishing for the impossible, what must be going through her young mind? "You see, little one, when we hit the ground, the body of the airplane must have become twisted, or maybe something blocked the door. Anyway, it jammed, and everybody who tried to go that way couldn't get out."

"My mommy," she whispered.

He could only nod, looking away to keep her from seeing his distress. She had enough to deal with without his losing control.

With a tug at his sleeve, Kris asked, "Which one's Auntie Rae's door?"

Again he had to clear his throat before he could speak. "The same one—the one closest to her seat."

"Kris." Rae took over as she walked around to kneel beside the chair that the girls shared. With an arm around each child, she said, "Baby, airplanes have instructions on what to do when something goes wrong. They tell passengers to go to the nearest emergency door, open it, and get out fast. That's exactly what your mom tried to do. I didn't follow the rules. It was dark, and I got lost. When I couldn't find Karen, I panicked, but I got really, really lucky because Daniel found me. He told me the way out."

"Oh." For a long time the solemn blond child stared at Daniel's sketch, until, at last, she sighed. Turning her troubled brown eyes on him, she asked, "Can I have this picture?"

"Of course." He suppressed the urge to gather her into his arms as he handed it to her.

Getting down from the chair, she turned to Rae. "Can I put it in my scrapbook?"

"Sure." Rae hugged both her nieces, but she lingered a bit longer with Kristen before she said, "Put it on my desk, and I'll help you with it later, okay?"

Staring at the drawing in her hands, the serious little girl never looked up as she walked slowly from the kitchen with Erin right on her heels.

Crossing his arms on the table in front of him, Daniel leaned forward to rest his head on them, asking quietly, "How do you think they took it?"

"Hard to tell about Kris." Rae got to her feet, placing an arm around his shoulders. "I don't think Erin paid any attention to anything except that you fly planes. Even if she did, she probably didn't grasp much of it."

Straightening up, he pulled Rae into his lap and buried his face in her shoulder. "Kristen understood, though. Every word."

Giving him a comforting hug, she said softly, "I'm sorry, Daniel. I should have told her about it a long time ago, but she never asked before. If Steve hadn't butted in, it might have been years before she got curious."

Raising his head, he found himself looking into eyes disconcertingly like Kristen's as he ran his fingers through the honey-colored silk that framed her delicate features. Drawing her mouth down to his, he savored her taste and touch for a moment before releasing her.

"Do you have any idea how much I love you?" he murmured as he gently stroked her cheek.

Covering his hand with hers, she pressed it snugly to her face. "Enough to put yourself through hell for my girls. You could've told them to 'ask Auntie Rae' on your way out the door, but you didn't. Until today,

I thought I couldn't possibly love or respect you any more than I already did. I was wrong."

Her words filled him with a healing warmth, and trying to absorb as much solace from them as possible, he closed his eyes. When he opened them again, he glanced toward the door through which the girls had disappeared. "Think they're okay?"

Following the direction of his gaze, she moved from his lap to the chair the children had vacated. "Give them a few more minutes. Kris is a brooder. She needs time to work things through."

"Yeah." He sighed. "She might decide she never wants to set eyes on me again. Then what happens to you and me?"

Squeezing his hand, she said calmly, "Let's wait and see how she takes it. Kris has great instincts about people, and she likes you . . ."

Her voice dwindled off as Kristen walked slowly into the room. Stopping right in front of him, she looked up directly into his eyes and said in a whisper-soft voice, "Wasn't your fault, Mr. Daniel."

He scooped the little girl into his arms, lifting her from the floor as he kissed her cheek. Momentarily unable to speak, he could only hug her tightly to him.

When he said nothing, she began gently patting his back, comforting him with her child's imitation of Rae's soothing manner. "That's all right, Daniel. You didn't hurt anybody on purpose. And thank you for helping Auntie Rae."

Finding his voice at last, he managed a gravelly-sounding reply. "I'd never do anything to hurt you or Erin or Rae. I promise."

Although he loosened his hold, she made no attempt to move from his lap, even when Erin charged into the room carrying a clean sheet of typing paper and a red crayon.

Shoving the supplies at him, she demanded, "Make me a red plane, Dan-yul."

Happy to comply, he laid the paper flat on the table, smiling as he reached around Kristen and began to draw. When he completed the picture, he handed it to the red-haired youngster for her inspection.

"Look, Krissy," she shouted, apparently satisfied with his efforts. "I got one, too. I can put it on Auntie Rae's desk with yours."

Sliding down from his lap, Kristen answered, "I'll help," and both children scampered from the room.

With a deep sigh, he slumped into his chair as the enormous tension that had built throughout the unforeseen crisis rushed from his body.

Reaching for his hand, Rae asked, "Better?"

He closed his fingers around hers, squeezing gently. "Relieved."

"Kristen knows when you're being honest with her, and by telling her the truth, you won her respect. She dropped the 'Mr.' "

"I noticed," he said with a shrug. "Whatever that means."

"She doesn't need the distance anymore. She trusts you."

"Well, if I'm supposed to feel the whole thing was worth it," he said, unable to suppress a wry smile, "I guess I do."

"Good." Determination sparked in her eyes, and the set of her jaw confirmed it. "But it shouldn't have happened that way. I give you my word Steve won't cause any more problems."

"God, I hope not. That was the toughest thing I've ever had to do in my life." Getting to his feet, he drew her up into his arms and held her close for a few minutes. "Guess I should get going."

"Sorry Steve wrecked our plans for the weekend,

but you don't have to leave if you don't want to," she said, returning his embrace.

"You and the girls could use some time alone."

"And you need some space."

"It's not that, sweetheart. I only want—"

Stretching up on tiptoe, she stopped him with a kiss. "It's okay. I understand. Everybody needs a break now and then. If you start to miss us, though, we'll be here."

"I miss you already," he murmured. "But having your portrait hanging over my fireplace ought to help . . . if you were serious about giving it away."

She smiled. "Want me to have it delivered, or do you want it now?"

"Now."

"Then I'll help you get it down. Will it fit in your car?"

"I'll make it fit," he said as the two of them headed up the stairs.

Rae got the stepladder from the hall closet, and soon they had the heavy-framed portrait down and wrapped securely in a quilt. After a few more minutes and a little artful space management, he managed to get it safely into his car. Then, with a good-bye wave to Rae and the girls, he drove off with the cherished picture.

The rest of the weekend passed uneventfully, with neither of the girls exhibiting any aftereffects of the emotionally charged account of the tragic plane crash. Though Rae, too, remained outwardly calm, her anger at Steve persisted. By the time he arrived at his automobile dealership on Monday morning, she had already been waiting an hour and a half for him.

Not at all surprised that he hadn't managed to get to work until well after his sales staff had opened for business, she greeted him coolly when he finally sauntered in. "Have a late night, Steve?"

Although he looked surprised to see her, he covered his initial displeasure by putting on his used-car-dealer smile. "Rae." His tone matched his expression. "What an unexpected pleasure."

Refusing to play his silly game, she said bluntly, "We need to get a few things straight regarding the children."

With a nervous glance at his secretary, he quickly ushered her into his office. "Have a seat. Want some coffee?"

"No, thanks. I didn't drop by for a friendly chat."

He sat at his desk, using slow, deliberate movements as he lit a cigarette. Exhaling, he looked straight at her, all trace of cordiality gone from his face. "Get to the point."

Ignoring his attempt at intimidation, she took the chair across from him. "Two things. First, how dare you criticize my relationship with Daniel when you flaunt your affair with Cookie right under your daughters' noses?"

"Cookie didn't kill their mother."

"Neither did Daniel." She paused for a moment to get a grip on her temper. "I'm going to keep on seeing him. We're not going to let your nasty little tricks come between us."

Anger flashed in his ice-blue eyes, marring his otherwise perfect features. "Your obsession with that man sounds sick to me."

"What's sick is the way you used your own children to hurt him. You hit your mark, but you also hurt Erin and especially Kristen. Was getting back at him for some imagined wrong worth what you did to them?"

"Imagined?" he sneered. "Did I imagine that plane crash?"

"It wasn't his fault." Her temper cooled. The depth of sorrow she saw in his eyes had hardly lessened at all in the two years since Karen had died. Maybe he still needed a scapegoat. "I know it helps to have some-one to blame, but Daniel didn't do anything wrong. Even the NTSB says so."

"Tell that to your sister."

She flinched at his bitter words. "Okay, Steve, you made your point. Nothing's going to change your mind about Daniel, but you can't change my feelings for him, either. Let's call a truce where the children are concerned. Why involve them in this?"

"I told them the truth," he said defiantly. "What's wrong with that?"

"Daniel explained to them what happened." She leaned forward, intent on opening his eyes to the harm he'd caused his daughters. "They understood, and they believed him."

"Sure they did." He ran a hand through his hair. "By the time he got through messing with their minds, they probably thought he was the biggest hero this side of heaven."

"He didn't make himself out a hero, and he didn't soft-pedal the part he played in the accident." Frustrated, Rae could only repeat, "He told them what happened—exactly the way it happened. He's paid the price for not being psychic. Get off his back."

"I'll get off his back when he brings me back my wife." Stubbing out his cigarette, Steve got up and strode over to the window to stare out at the multicolored rows of shiny new cars. "I'll tell you something else, Rae. I don't want my kids around him anymore."

A vague uneasiness settled over her as the import of his words sunk in. "What do you mean?"

"Do I have to spell it out for you?" He laughed, and the nasty sound made her skin crawl.

"I guess you do," she almost whispered, feeling as though the breath had been knocked from her body. She couldn't take her eyes off him as he crossed back to his desk. Sinking into his leather office chair, he leaned forward, glaring at her, a cruel glint in his eyes.

"Listen closely, sister-in-law. My kids are not to have any further contact with your loser of a boyfriend. Got it?"

"But they can't help seeing him when he comes over."

With a cold smile, he said, "Don't use that stupid routine on me. Nobody who makes the kind of money you pull in from those cutesy little beauty salons of yours could be that dumb. You know what I'm saying. Do whatever you have to do to keep that murderer away from my kids." He relaxed back into his chair. "Looks like you have a decision to make."

She rose from her chair and, with as much dignity as she could muster, walked over to the door. Pausing, she turned to look at him. "Forget it, Steve. You can't bully me into ending my relationship with Daniel."

"No?" Placing both hands flat on his desk, he stood up and stared hard at her. "Then maybe it's time for *my* daughters to move back home with me."

The chill that started in the pit of her stomach spread throughout her body, numbing her mind as well as her fingers as her worst nightmare became reality. Staggering back against the door, she grasped the knob for support as she struggled desperately to present a calm facade. "You can't mean that."

"But, dear sister, I do."

"They've lived with me for two years—most of their lives. To move them now . . . they'd be so confused and hurt. Have you considered Kris and Erin at all, or is harming Daniel all that matters to you?"

Smiling triumphantly, he sat back down. "You wound me to the quick, Rae. Of course I'm thinking of the girls. How could I live with myself if I allowed them to continue to hang around your lousy pilot boyfriend?" Gesturing toward the chair she had vacated a few minutes earlier, he added, "Sit down. Two reasonable adults ought to be able to work something out—if we try hard enough."

Unsure her quaking knees would hold her up if she let go of the doorknob, she took a moment to steel herself for Steve's next maneuver. After fortifying herself as best she could under the circumstances, she walked back toward his desk. Taking the chair he indicated, she stared hard at him, unable to shake the feeling that she had never met him before.

How was it possible to know someone so well and so little at the same time? What had happened to the man Karen had loved, the man who had fathered two such delightful children? Had losing his wife warped Steve into some kind of unfeeling ogre, or had he always been capable of using his daughters in such a despicable way? If so, it seemed unlikely that Rae wouldn't have known. Yet what did anyone ever know about a brother-in-law, except what one's sister chose to reveal?

Fascinated, she continued studying him as she said, "What do you have in mind?"

He lit another cigarette. "Let's consider your options." He held up his index finger. "One, you stop dating that jerk." His second finger joined the first. "Two, the girls come to live with me." His ring finger came up in order. "Three, we come to some sort of accommodation."

"Such as?"

He laughed that bone-chilling laugh again. "Think, Rae. What do you have more of than you need—something that might persuade me to turn a blind eye to that sordid relationship you're engaged in?" He paused for a fraction of a second. "Give up? It's green; it's easily portable; with it, a man can get whatever he wants."

"Money."

"Bingo."

"If you're in a financial bind, I'll be glad to lend you whatever you need. You don't have to use threats."

"A loan?" He shook his head in disbelief. "You still don't get it, do you? I don't need a loan. What I want, well, let's call it a gift—a gift I'm sure you'll want to keep on giving at, say, monthly intervals."

Amazed, she had to concentrate to keep her mouth from dropping open. "You'd sell your interest in your daughters?"

Exhaling a thin trail of smoke, he leaned back in his chair and propped his feet up on one corner of his desk. "You know what they say about every man having his price."

"And yours is?"

"We'll discuss that after I've had a chance to weigh the value of what you'll be getting against what I give up by looking the other way regarding your affairs."

Sick at the casual way he bargained away his children's lives, she said, "Karen would have been appalled by what you're doing."

In one swift motion, he jerked his feet off the desk and sat up straight in his chair, fixing her with a cold stare that contrasted dramatically with the red-hot flush that blotched his face. "What the hell would you know about Karen? She got all the brains, the looks, and the personality in your family. You're nothing but a bunch of leftovers. And you're not even smart enough to know it."

"Oh, I know it," Rae said quietly, swallowing hard at his stinging assessment. "I've always known it, but it never mattered because Karen didn't seem to notice."

"No," he agreed. "And I never understood her devotion to you."

"Neither did I, but I know if she were alive, she'd never stand for what you're doing."

"Well, she's not alive, thanks to your boyfriend. Now I want what I'm due."

"And you don't care who pays, not even if that ends up being Karen's little girls. You make me sick."

"Do I?"

He smiled, chilling her to the bone.

Crushing out his cigarette, he lit another before continuing. "That's too bad, since we'll be working so closely together in the future. I expect to hear from you at least once a month, and you never know when I might drop in to see my kids."

Gathering all her courage, she sat up straight, looking him in the eye as she said, "Your blackmail won't work. I'm going to file for custody of Kris and Erin, something I should've done a long time ago."

"But you didn't." His expression didn't change, and he didn't so much as move a muscle. "I might even have gone for that before. Now it's too late. Your lawyer'll confirm that. Mine has. They're still *my* kids under *my* custody, no matter where they've been living recently. No judge or jury is going to change that."

"Unless I tell them about the little scheme you outlined for me this morning."

"Tell 'em. I'll say you're lying. Your word against mine, and everybody'll believe me, the grieving husband who needed only temporary help with his poor, motherless children. Now their bad old auntie Rae is trying to steal them away from me. I can charm the pants off anyone when I choose to. I can even cry on cue." His cold smile changed to a threatening glare. "If you cross me, I won't hesitate to spread your name and reputation all over Texas—maybe the world, if your family name leaks to the media. Just think, you could be the new queen of tabloid cover stories."

"What makes you think I won't bring up your relationship with Cookie?"

"What of it? Grief made me do it. Besides, no matter how many bras have been burned, society still accepts that sort of thing from a man far more readily than from a woman, and you'd have to show proof."

"The way you flaunt it, that shouldn't be a problem. Even the girls know about Cookie and you."

"Would you put them on the witness stand to be cross-examined by my attorney? I don't think so. Auntie Rae would never do that to her beloved nieces."

Her ability to fight back abandoned her as his words hit their mark. He had her figured down to the last detail. She would never let him drag the girls through a bitter custody battle, even if it meant her losing them.

He went on. "Daddy would, though. I wouldn't hesitate to put them on the stand so they could tell the world about you and your lover. What do you think a jury would make of that cozy little scene we walked in on last Saturday morning? Can't you nearly see the disgust on their faces? And when they award custody to the kids' natural father, I'll make sure you never see them again."

"I can see appealing to your better side would be a waste of time, since you don't have one."

"Good shot. I'll remember that when I make out my new budget. You'd better be nice to me, Rae, or believe me, you'll regret it. Imagine Cookie as stepmother."

The very thought made her sick to her stomach, and, desperate for a breath of air tainted by neither Steve's cigarette smoke nor his odious threats and insults, she rose wordlessly from her chair. Turning to leave, she opened the door as Steve's parting shot reached her.

"I'll go over those figures we discussed and get back to you," he called out loudly enough for his secretary to hear. "You can count on it."

His final threat caused her but a moment's hesitation before she exited his office, closing the door firmly behind her.

ELEVEN

Rae pulled into the parking lot, relieved to find a space near the mall entrance not far from her studio. For a moment she sat absolutely still, gripping the steering wheel as if, by refusing to let go, she could somehow nullify the threat to her nieces and to her peace of mind.

She must find a way to stop Steve from taking the girls away from her. Such a move would cause irreparable damage to Kristen and Erin unless their father made drastic changes in the way he conducted his affairs, but Steve would never alter his lifestyle to include his children. He would consider them unwelcome intruders in his home, and he would make no effort whatsoever to keep them from knowing how he felt. For Kris, it would be a tragic, ego-destroying situation. Erin would never stop fighting for attention, with no chance of ever winning it. Rae couldn't let that happen to her nieces— no matter what the cost.

With new resolve, she got out of her car. First she would contact her attorney. With a clearer idea of her standing in the matter, she would know better how to proceed. Preoccupied with fashioning a strategy for countering Steve's plot, she headed straight for her office.

As she entered the lobby, Jenna glanced up at the clock. "Judging by the time and the expression on your face, I'd say you had a tough weekend."

"I've had better."

"Myself." Leaning on the front counter, Jenna said, "Eddie from Lamaze class called Saturday to invite me and my cousin Barb to his home for dinner."

"Eddie?"

"The guy who's been putting the make on me."

"Oh. Right."

"Before I could think of a way to get out of it, he said Barb had already accepted for both of us. I almost made up an excuse, anyway, until he put his wife on the line. She sounded so enthusiastic, I didn't have the heart to turn her down. It's next Saturday, so that's another weekend down the tubes. Can you believe it? He expects his wife to cook dinner for the woman he's been running like a greyhound after. Nobody should put up with that kind of garbage."

"No," Rae answered distractedly as she started toward the office, making her way through the bustling makeup room.

Following her, Jenna prodded, "So tell me, what has you in the dumps?"

Motioning Jenna into the office, Rae closed the door behind her. "Steve's threatening to take the girls away from me."

"Oh, no." Jenna threw her arms around her friend. "Why'd you let me go on and on about that stupid dinner invitation when you had real problems? How can I help?"

Rae returned Jenna's hug, glad for her support. "Take care of things here. Call in a replacement for me today, and schedule around me for the next few weeks. If you have to, hire another part-timer, or give anybody who wants it overtime to pick up the slack."

"No problem. Sherry and Ken have been asking for more hours, anyway."

"I'll do the paperwork, but I want you to handle everything else." Sinking into her chair, Rae looked up at her steadfast friend and invaluable colleague. "Am I dumping too much on you this time?"

Jenna shook her head. "I'll take care of the paperwork, too, if you want me to."

Rae smiled. "I knew I could count on you. I'll never forget the way you single-handedly kept both stores going after we lost Karen."

An embarrassed flush covered Jenna's face. "Stop it. You'll make me cry."

"Please don't, or you'll set me off." Rae reached for the telephone receiver. "And I don't want to be bawling when I talk to my attorney."

"Good luck," Jenna said, leaving the office.

The conversation with her lawyer failed to produce the answers Rae hoped for. On the contrary, everything her attorney told her reinforced Steve's claims. With all the cards stacked in his favor, what options were left to her? What would it take to ransom her nieces?

A tap on the door pulled her back from the brink of despair.

"Yes?" she called out.

Opening the door a crack, Jenna stuck her head into the room. "How'd it go?"

"A custody battle's out of the question. It'd be a living hell for the girls, and Steve would probably win."

"What's happened to common sense in our court system?" Jenna asked in an indignant tone before abruptly changing the subject. "You've got a call holding on line two. It's long distance from Detroit."

"Who do I know in Detroit?"

"Your mother." Looking contrite, Jenna explained, "I told her you were here before I found out who she was."

"Forget it. She'd have tracked me down sooner or later."

Jenna left, closing the door as Rae reached for the telephone.

"Darling," Edie gushed in her usual sugary tone. "How are you?"

With a weary sigh, Rae replied, "What do you want, Edie?"

"A bit of civility would be nice."

Wishing to avoid battle on a second front, Rae managed to keep most of the sarcasm out of her voice as she spoke. "I'm fine. And you?"

"Remarkably well, dear. Our speaking tour is going marvelously."

"How nice. What do you want?"

Mollified by the exchange of even the most basic niceties, Edie launched into her reason for calling. "Nick and I have spoken with Steve, dear. That young man is extremely concerned about the effect your relationship with your pilot friend is having on our granddaughters."

Rae didn't bother to hide her annoyance as she said, "If that 'young man' had one tenth the integrity, compassion, or courage of my 'pilot friend,' he wouldn't be using you to try to influence me."

"But, darling, he's at the end of his rope. If you had listened to reason, he would never have involved your father and me."

"What reason wouldn't I listen to?"

"Anything regarding your personal affairs, of course. You must stop seeing your . . . that . . . person. Can you imagine how it would affect the children to find out that the man you are running around with killed their mother?"

"In the first place, Daniel and I have never run around anything or anywhere together." Sick of Edie's syrupy, asinine defense of the snake she called her son-in-law, Rae erupted. "As for Kris and Erin, they already know about the accident. Steve told them, and after he'd done his best to hurt them with his lies, Daniel talked to them. He was gentle and honest. He did everything he could to protect them from any more pain. I don't want to hear another word against Daniel. You don't know him. And you sure don't know Steve."

Sounding indignant, Edie said, "I knew you would react this way, yet I felt obligated to make an effort. The potential harm to those darling children outweighed all my misgivings. From the beginning, your father and I questioned the advisability of their living with you. Your lack of experience in raising children—"

"*You* are going to give *me* advice on child rearing?" Rae interrupted, unable to keep from laughing at the absurdity of Nick and Edie counseling anyone on parenting. "That's a good one. All you ever did was call a servant to take care of your children's needs, and even that ended when you decided to run off and play savior of the world.

"For your information, Steve's the worst excuse for a father I can imagine, and nobody would make a better parent than Daniel. Of course, my opinion won't mean much to you, the self-appointed experts at everything. I'm warning you, though, I won't let you help destroy a second generation with your ignorance. Stay out of this."

Without another word, she slammed the receiver back into its cradle. How bad could a day get? Nearly leaping from her chair, she rushed out of the office, as if putting distance between her and the telephone could somehow soften the ominous message behind that phone call. By involving her parents, Steve had given notice that he intended to use every method at his disposal to achieve his ends. He would stop at nothing.

"Jenna, may I have a word with you?" Rae asked, amazed that she didn't sound like a babbling idiot by now.

"Sure." Jenna excused herself from the customer in her makeup chair and met Rae at the front desk. "What's up?"

"My dander. If I don't get out of here, I'll go stark raving mad."

"Take off."

"Will that leave you in a bind for lunchtime relief?"

Jenna shook her head. "Most everybody's already gone. Besides, I called Sherry in. She'll be here any minute."

Without further delay, Rae left the studio, but when she got into her truck, she had no idea where to find respite from this waking nightmare. Ten minutes on the road, however, revealed her destination—the flight academy.

The mere thought of seeing Daniel made her feel better. If anyone could keep her from giving in to utter hopelessness, he could, and no one would be more supportive. Her spirits lifted somewhat during the long drive to the academy. But as she parked the Blazer in front of his building, her uncertainty returned.

Unsure how he would feel about having her drop by unannounced at his place of employment, she approached the reception desk with some hesitation.

"I'd like to see Daniel MacKay, please," she said in answer to the receptionist's questioning glance.

The young woman checked a list before replying, "He's signed out to the flight simulator for the rest of the afternoon."

Feeling as though someone had pulled the rug out from under her for about the tenth time that day, Rae couldn't keep her disappointment from showing.

Quickly, the receptionist added, "He might not have started yet. Let me page him to make sure."

Grateful, Rae watched intently as the personable young woman picked up the telephone receiver, dialed, and entered a series of numbers before hanging up again.

"Why don't you have a seat while you wait?" she said, directing Rae to a group of chairs near the floor-to-ceiling windows that brightened one end of the lobby. Overlooking a small but restful-looking parklike area surrounded by multistoried buildings, they framed a peaceful scene in counterpoint to the high-tech, high-stress business going on all around it.

Rae, however, was too agitated to sit still. Oblivious to the comings and goings around her, she alternately paced the small waiting area and stood, leaning against a marble pillar and tapping one foot on the thick-piled carpet. When Daniel hadn't responded to his page after ten minutes, she gave up.

With a smile of thanks for the receptionist, she turned to go, but as she reached for the door handle, the sound of Daniel's voice stopped her.

"Got a message for me, Nancy?" Catching sight of Rae, he broke into a smile, and not bothering to wait for the girl's reply, he said, "Rae! What a nice surprise."

Relief flooded through her. Although she had hoped to see Daniel, she hadn't realized how much she had counted on it. Walking over to him, she said softly, "I didn't think you were going to answer your page."

"I was nearby, so I decided to pick up my message in person." He chuckled. "Wasn't all that long, was it?"

"I thought you were in the simulator."

"Will be." He checked his watch. "In about fifteen minutes."

To cover her disappointment, she tried to smile. In

fifteen minutes, she couldn't even begin to relate the unhappy events that had filled her morning, and she had no intention of interfering with his work. "I won't keep you, then."

"Something wrong?"

She shrugged. "Nothing that can't wait."

"Sure?"

She nodded.

Again he glanced at his watch. "Gotta get going, sweetheart. Sorry."

With another forced smile, she turned to leave, but he grabbed her arm.

"Walk over with me," he suggested. "We'll talk on the way."

The receptionist handed her a visitor's pass as Daniel took her arm to guide her from the lobby.

"Thought you worked on Mondays," he said as they crossed the pleasant little courtyard to an adjacent building.

With a nod, she answered, "Usually, but today I'm taking the afternoon off."

"Must be serious for you to be neglecting your business."

"Just playing hooky." The lie nearly stuck in her throat.

He stopped at the entrance to the building housing the simulators, and without releasing her arm, he leaned against the doorjamb. "Something tells me this isn't a good time to be locking myself in a simulator for several hours."

"You'll be making judgments in there that could make or break careers, and you shouldn't have anything else on your mind while you do it." She covered his hand with hers, resisting by the slimmest of margins the temptation to throw herself into his arms and pour out her problems. "I'm all right."

"Okay, for now. Later, I expect to hear what this is

all about.'' Lifting her hand to his lips, he kissed her fingertips lightly before disappearing through the door.

After retracing her steps, she returned her visitor's pass and left the academy. Driving away, she again had no clear destination in mind until, impelled by an overwhelming urge to see her nieces, she turned toward home. The distance added by leaving from the flight academy almost doubled her regular commute, and although she urged her truck along the highway as fast as the law allowed, the miles passed so slowly that it took forever to reach the Decatur city limits. From there she was just minutes from home, and she sighed with relief when she passed the courthouse and turned into her street.

The moment she rounded the corner, however, she sighted Steve's car parked in front of her home. An unexpected visit from him could only mean trouble, and it made her sick to consider what his motives for dropping by unannounced might be. Had he planned to spirit the girls out of the house without her knowledge? Near panic, she pulled into her drive. Delaying no longer than it took to turn off the engine, she raced through the back door to find Steve sitting alone at her kitchen table, devouring a huge platterful of leftovers.

Looking up at her abrupt entrance, he grinned. "Didn't have time for lunch today, so I made myself at home. Knew you wouldn't mind."

With her heart in her mouth, she demanded, "Where are the girls?"

"Upstairs," he replied with his mouth full. "Where'd you think they were?"

"And Elena?"

"Gave her the afternoon off. You haven't told her about our new arrangement yet, have you? She didn't ask a single question when I volunteered to stay with the kids for the rest of the day."

"What do you want?" Hoping to keep him from

knowing how much his prank had upset her, she turned her back to him, busying herself with rearranging the items on the counter to make a place for her purse.

But he saw through her pretense. "Scared you, huh? Well, you had it coming. Maybe you'll take my little proposal more seriously now. Anytime I want to, I can waltz right in here, get my kids, and be long gone before you know what hit you. Even if you found out about it, you couldn't stop me. Law's on my side."

"You've had your fun." Still standing, she faced him. "Now, get out."

"Didn't my little demonstration impress you at all, Rae? Don't push me into arranging a stronger one, because I'm not bluffing. If I have to prove it, you'll be sorry. Then it'll be too late."

"You made your point. What more do you want?"

"Sit down." Motioning toward the chair across from him, he waited for her to comply, pushing aside his half-empty plate before shoving a piece of paper at her. "That's what it'll cost you to keep the kids. *My* kids."

She needed no reminder of her nieces' parentage. Bitterly conscious of who exercised control over their lives, she reached for the paper that lay on the table. Though fully aware that she would find nothing in Steve's list of demands that would allay her fears for the girls, she couldn't stop hoping for a miracle as she skipped over the detailed accounting of his expenses to focus on the bottom line.

In spite of her attempt to cover any expression of emotion, a gasp escaped her throat. "You can't be serious."

"But, my dear sister-in-law, I am." He leaned back, balancing his chair on two legs. "Very serious. And don't try haggling. I'm not going to lower my asking price."

Contemptuously, she tossed his ridiculous list back at him. "You've overestimated my income. That wouldn't leave me enough to support a hummingbird, much less two children.''

"Oh, Rae.'' He rocked forward, returning the chair to its normal position as he shook his head in mock distress. "I won't penalize you for trying to put one over on me—this time. But be very careful before you try that again. You're not sharp enough to pull it off. Have you forgotten that I've got access to Karen's financial records? I used those figures, multiplied by two to account for her half of the earnings from the New Orleans store. That doesn't even take into account inflation or the increase in business over the past two years. But it's still a tidy sum, and it's no more than I'm due, since that clever arrangement the two of you worked out kept me from sharing your little windfall.''

"We had a standard partnership agreement with right of survivorship.''

"Whatever you call it, it worked out pretty good for you.''

Tears momentarily blurred her vision as she stared at him in disbelief. "If you think I'd have traded Karen's life for any amount of money, you've lost your mind. Every single penny that would've been her share of profits goes into a trust fund for Kristen and Erin, and you know it.''

"So that leaves me the odd man out. Anyway, if you'll check my figures, you'll see I allowed for that.''

"You sure haven't deducted one red cent for the support I provided your daughters over the past two years without any help from you.''

"My, my. Does this mean that Auntie Rae begrudges her precious little nieces a comfortable living?''

"It means that their freeloading father doesn't know the meaning of responsibility any better than he does decency.'' No longer able to contain her anger at his cavalier attitude toward his children, Rae let her feelings spill out, unguarded. "I'd give everything I own to keep Kristen and Erin out of your reach. It'd break their hearts to know how little you care for them— that to you they're only property to be bargained away. They'd never understand it. Even after hearing you say it, I still can't believe you'd deprive them of the basic necessities just to support your high-roller image."

"Believe it. Anyway, it won't be so bad. They'll have to eat tuna instead of steak for a while. So what? They could use a good lesson in survival after the way you've spoiled them."

"Be reasonable, if that's possible with those dollar signs in your eyes. I don't have a choice, so I'm willing to deal, but you've got to leave me enough to take care of the girls. You can have every penny over that that I can scrape up."

"Either I get what I want, or I get my precious babies back. See, you were wrong. You do have a choice after all."

He grinned humorlessly, his expression suggestive of a bloodsucking parasite as he leaned across the table toward her.

Almost licking his lips, he went on. "If it's the amount that's bothering you and not the principle, then maybe you can satisfy me some other way. Help me get a good settlement—my definition, not yours—from New World Airways."

"How? That trial might not come up for years."

His eyes widened. "You don't know, do you? It's set for next month. The sixteenth, to be exact."

Stunned, she said nothing.

Taking advantage of her silence, he said, "All you have to do is show up in court looking like a grieving widow and convince the jury that your poor, heartbroken old brother-in-law deserves a bundle for the loss of his beloved wife. You don't even have to come up with a good story. Cry a lot and keep pointing at that lousy pilot. Everybody in the courtroom will think you're saying he killed your dear, sweet sister. The pity you'll get with that helpless, idiotic look of yours will include me as well. Make it good enough, and I just might let you off the hook."

"Now I see why you dragged Daniel into this. I couldn't figure out why you pretended at first that you only wanted us to stop seeing each other when you meant all along to use the children to blackmail me. You linked him to your dirty little scheme because you want me to make him your scapegoat. That's why you made it a choice between my nieces and the man I love—to find out how easily I'd betray him. When I didn't react the way you hoped I would, you knew it'd take your nastiest tricks to get what you wanted, so you upped the ante. It's still a choice between Daniel and the girls. You've just raised the stakes."

"So poor, dumb Rae finally figured it out. Well, don't think I won't call you on it. For once, don't be stupid."

She laughed humorlessly. "Oh, believe me, I've overestimated your sense of decency for the last time. Money's your god. It doesn't matter how you get it or where it comes from, but you'd rather have the airline pay you off because they've got deeper pockets than I do. A leech like you doesn't care who or what he destroys on the way to his sick victory. Nothing, not your children, not even Karen's memory, means anything to you."

His eyes glittering with anger, he leaned so close to her that she could feel his breath on her face. "Watch what you say, Rae. Remember what's at stake. Cross me, and the kids come to live with me. Got it?"

"Daddy, I don't want to live with you." Kristen's tiny voice trembled as she walked slowly into the kitchen. "I want to stay with Auntie Rae."

"Who cares what you want? I make the decisions for you and your sister."

With his eyes fixed on Rae, Steve missed seeing Kristen's crushed expression as tears began trickling down her cheeks. Rae saw it, though, and her heart broke for her niece.

Reaching to gather Kristen into her arms, she glared at the unfeeling man across from her. "You've done enough damage for one day. Get out."

"Sure, but we'll talk again, Auntie Rae. You have my word on it." With no sign that his daughter's unhappiness meant anything at all to him, he stalked out of the room.

The moment Steve disappeared through the door, Kristen burst into sobs, her little body shaking. She spoke almost incoherently, her words coming out in ragged gasps. "Auntie . . . Rae, I . . . don't want . . . to live with . . . Daddy. Let us stay with you. Please. We'll be good. I promise we'll be good."

Unshed tears choked Rae's voice as she held her little niece close, whispering, "Baby, you're always good. Don't worry. Everything'll be all right. You'll see."

Drawn by the commotion in the kitchen, Erin skipped into the room. Stopping in her tracks at the sight of her sister's distress, she promptly burst into tears of sympathy, and though she didn't know what had caused Kristen's uncontrollable weeping, her confusion at having walked into such an alarming scene was real.

With Kristen still in her arms, Rae slid out of her chair to sit on the floor and drew Erin, too, onto her lap. Holding both her crying nieces in a tight hug, she struggled mightily to keep from joining them, but she knew her tears would only upset them more, and that was the last thing any of them needed.

How long she remained sitting on the kitchen floor, comforting her nieces, she didn't know. Nor had she the slightest idea how she would keep the promises she had made. The one thing she knew for certain was that she would fight to her last breath to keep Karen's children safe from their father's greed.

TWELVE

Daniel strolled aimlessly along the sidewalk around the Decatur town square, paying no more attention to his actions than necessary to prevent being run over when crossing the street from one block to another. Lost in thought, he stopped to stare, unseeing, into a plate-glass window fronting one of the businesses that bordered the Wise County Courthouse.

Now what? His first reaction to overhearing Rae's blackmailing brother-in-law threaten her had been to rush in and settle the matter with his fists. The satisfaction of finally getting to knock the smug expression off Steve's face would have been short-lived, though, if the smarmy, yuppie-looking jerk proved to be stronger than he appeared. Besides, throwing each other around Rae's kitchen wouldn't have accomplished anything except to break some dishes and scare the kids. So he'd opted for his second plan—to withdraw unnoticed until he could come up with a third plan.

But no brilliant scheme presented itself. Nothing, that is, except compromising New World's defense of Steve's lawsuit. As a party to the case, he was privy to much of the information uncovered by the airline's investigators, and they had learned enough about Steve's shady business dealings to persuade the proper authorities to initiate a formal investigation. The outcome would likely mean jail time for him, and even a child's father might have difficulty retaining custody while sitting in a prison cell.

Rae, however, didn't know how hollow Steve's threats were. By the time the pertinent facts came out in court next month, whom would she blame for prolonging her journey through hell? With her loyalties already strained to the breaking point, a month would seem interminable, and how, after enduring such torment, could she be expected to understand Daniel's reasons for allowing it to continue when he had known all along about Steve's vulnerability? In her mind, how would his oath to maintain confidentiality stack up against her fear of losing contact with her sister's children?

The shimmering image of a new, spotless black Camaro swam across the glass in front of him, and he turned in time to see self-satisfaction clearly written on Steve's face as he drove out of town. Too impressed with himself to notice anything else, the worthless bum hadn't seen Daniel. Just as well. A brawl in Rae's kitchen would have been bad enough. Engaging in such behavior less than fifteen steps from the courthouse would probably have landed them both in jail.

Daniel headed across the square to his own car. With Rae's home but a few blocks away, he'd better come up with a plan soon.

Once there, he parked on the street, but he bypassed the front walk to follow the long driveway toward the hazy semicircle of light emanating from the kitchen door. Taking the back steps two at a time, he knocked, calling out, "It's me, Rae."

"Come on in."

The plaintive note in her voice tugged at his heart,

and he entered to find her sitting in the middle of the kitchen floor, cuddling both her sniffling nieces. From the looks of things, Steve hadn't spared even the little girls his singular brand of nastiness.

Without a word, Daniel sat down beside them, crossing his legs Indian fashion as he lifted Erin from Rae's lap into his own. Apparently unconcerned by the change of nurturers, the normally spunky little redhead snuggled into his arms.

Looking up at him with a woeful gaze, she slipped her thumb from her mouth long enough to say, between hiccups, "I been cryin', Daniel."

"So I see." Taking a clean handkerchief from his pocket, he wiped her nose as he asked, "Now, what would make two sweet little girls like you cry?"

Erin shrugged. "Dunno. Krissy was cryin' first."

Rae gestured toward his handkerchief, and he handed it to her, watching as she gently cleaned Kristen's face. Though the tears could simply be wiped away, the child's distress wasn't so easily dealt with.

Turning her large, troubled brown eyes on him, Kristen answered the question he'd asked Erin. "Daddy said we have to go live with him."

"Unh-*unh*." Erin shot out of Daniel's lap to stand with her hands on her hips, facing her sister.

Kristen nodded. "Didn't he, Auntie Rae?"

Before Rae could reply, however, Erin shook her head, stamping one foot in a display of defiance. "Well, I'm not goin' to. I'm gonna stay here and live with Auntie Rae forever."

"Of course you are," Rae said, but her tone had a hollow ring that sounded anything but confident.

Squatting beside her sister, Erin patted Kristen's head as she had seen Rae do. "See? You don't have to cry anymore, Krissy. And I'm hungry."

Rae hugged the little girl. "I'm not surprised. It's

way past your dinnertime. How about you, Kris? Feel like eating?''

Kristen shook her head.

Gently teasing, Rae coaxed, "Well, okay. Guess we'll just have to let Erin starve.''

At Erin's howl of protest, Kristen nearly smiled, but she remained silent.

In the absence of a better idea, Daniel offered his own suggestion. "Let's try the restaurant on the corner of the square. It was open when I passed by a little while ago.''

"Mattie's," both girls said in unison.

"How's the food?" Since they obviously knew the restaurant, he deferred to their judgment.

"We love Mattie's," Erin answered enthusiastically. "Please, Auntie Rae?''

Rae shrugged. "Whatever you and Kris decide.''

Resorting to wheedling, Erin gave her sister a look that could wring tears from a turnip. "Pleeease, Krissy?''

Kristen nodded her acceptance.

Getting to her feet, Rae checked both girls' hands and faces. "We've got some washing up to do, then, and your hair's a mess.''

Obediently, her nieces started for the back stairs, but when Rae followed, Kristen stopped her.

Looking intently at her aunt, she said, "That's okay, Auntie Rae. You stay here and keep Daniel company. We can do it all by ourself.''

Rae opened her mouth as if to argue but closed it again without saying a word, then motioned the children to go on. Turning, she reached a hand to Daniel, and he gratefully took it, pulling himself up from the floor before he drew her into his arms.

"You can't imagine what's been going on here today," she whispered, her dilemma echoed in her troubled voice.

"Oh, I think I can." He held her in a loose embrace, stroking her hair as she buried her face in the crook of his neck. "You were pretty upset out at the flight academy this afternoon, so I found another instructor who could fill in for me and came straight over here. But Steve got here first. Back door was open, and I could hear you talking."

Clearly taken off guard, she looked up at him. "What did you hear?"

"Enough to know he's trying to blackmail you. I left before he got the children so worked up." Taking her face between his hands, he stroked her temples with his thumbs. "I felt like knocking his lights out, but I didn't want to make things worse. And since my self-control was all but used up, I thought I'd better cool off someplace else. Hope that wasn't a mistake. He didn't try to hurt you . . . I mean, physically, or anything, did he?"

She shook her head. "That's not his style, leaving marks. Anyway, I'm glad you didn't come in. I'd have probably ended up crying, and that would've made his day." Her words dwindled off as she squeezed her eyes shut. Leaning forward to rest her forehead on his chest, she whispered hoarsely, "Oh, God, Daniel, what am I going to do?"

"Nothing," he said, hoping she wouldn't pick up on his too-confident tone. "Just don't let him take the girls—not for any reason—and everything'll be all right."

Raising her head, she looked up at him, her eyes filled with a mixture of curiosity and admiration. "How can you be so sure?"

He trained his eyes on the floor to avoid meeting hers as he struggled to come up with an explanation that would account for his attitude without divulging too much. His heart told him to hold back nothing. His brain reminded him of his legal obligation.

The sound of the children's footsteps in the hall kept him from having to answer, but he knew it was a temporary reprieve. After dinner, when Rae's nieces had gone to bed, he would have to explain. He hoped that by then he would have found a solution they all could live with.

"Okeydoke, we're ready," Erin shouted, demanding their attention as the girls came through the door.

Shooting one last glance at Daniel, Rae whispered, "We'll talk later." Raising her voice, she turned to her nieces. "Then let's go."

Rae ushered everyone out of the house and locked up behind her before they started out for the restaurant. Even after dark the air remained hot and muggy, closing in around them as they set off on foot. The oppressive atmosphere wore on Daniel's nerves.

Aware that he sounded proprietary and stuffy, he couldn't stop himself from saying, "Hope you don't go walking around by yourselves at night like this very often."

"Only when we go to Mattie's," Rae said calmly, the smile in her eyes not quite reaching her lips. "Don't worry I'll protect you from the bogeyman."

How she found the spirit to make a joke after the day she'd had, he would never know, but if she wanted him to laugh, he had no intention of disappointing her. Grinning, he answered, "Then hold my hand so I won't get scared."

Taking her hand in his, he kept an eye on the girls as they skipped on ahead, pausing at street corners until he and Rae caught up to help them across. Watching them now, he saw little evidence of the upset they had experienced earlier, but Rae's distracted silence told him she hadn't forgotten it. Filled with a need to protect her, he tightened his fingers around hers.

The short walk to Mattie's took no more than ten minutes, and they soon found themselves seated comfortably in a booth beside a window that overlooked Main Street, enjoying the closest thing to a Texas-style, home-cooked meal he'd had outside his mother's country kitchen in a long while. With Kristen and Rae sitting across from him and Erin, he had the perfect vantage point from which to gauge Rae's state of mind. Though she remained quieter than usual, he would have noticed nothing out of the ordinary if not for the piercing gaze she fixed on him from time to time.

Kristen, too, watched him with uncommon interest. Studying him across the table, she picked at her food, saying little except to ask a question now and then in an apparent effort to fill the conversational lapses with her child's version of small talk.

Erin alone seemed completely recovered from the afternoon's turmoil as she prattled away, managing to down her old-fashioned hamburger, all her French fries, and half of Kristen's before she finally finished her meal.

Eventually, however, overeating along with the stifling summer evening and the late hour subdued even Erin's usual exuberance, and she whined, "Take me, Daniel," the moment they left the restaurant. Happy to oblige, he lifted her into his arms for the walk home, and by the time they had covered the few blocks back from Mattie's, she had fallen sound asleep.

"Want me to take her upstairs?" he asked as Rae opened the front door.

She shook her head. "I'll do it." Closing the door after them, she turned to take Erin from his arms. "But don't leave. We have to talk."

He didn't need a reminder of the emotional tightrope he would have to negotiate if he hoped to retain a place in her affections. He had thought of little else since overhearing Steve's ultimatum. Still, as he followed Kristen into the living room, he didn't have the slightest idea what he would say to Rae.

"You look tired, Kris," he said, joining the little girl on the sofa. "Why don't you go up to bed? You don't have to baby-sit me."

Without so much as cracking a smile at his feeble joke, she nodded, staring straight into his eyes with absolute sincerity as she said, "You can come live with us if you want to, Daniel. Eri and me won't mind."

In a flash of understanding, he realized that the questions she had so carefully spaced throughout dinner hadn't been small talk at all. She was interviewing him as a prospective housemate. Stunned, he could only stare at her as he tried to remember her questions as well as his answers.

Did he like Decatur, their house, picnics? Yes. *Did he get lonely living all alone?* More lately than he used to. *Would he like to have a garden, a big yard, an attic?* Sometimes. *How did he feel about little girls?* He loved the two having dinner with him.

If he hadn't been so preoccupied with finding a way to minimize this new tension between him and Rae, he would have noticed the direction the child's conversation had taken. Even distracted, he should have recognized the pattern.

"Don't you want to come live with us?" Kristen's voice trembled as she searched his face for the answer he hadn't yet managed to put into words.

Stalling a moment longer, he cleared his throat. "Kris, it's not a question of whether I *want* to live here—"

"But you like it here, you said so."

"Sure I do, but as much as I like you girls and Rae and your home and everything, I can't move in"—he snapped his fingers—"just like that. Rae and I haven't even talked about anything like that yet."

"Auntie Rae won't mind. I promise."

"Little one," he began, but the desperation behind Kristen's words raised a lump in his throat. Swallowing hard, he tried again. "Kris, one day, if I'm very lucky, it might happen that I come to live here, but these things take time. First, Rae and I would have to get married. . . ."

"That's okay. You can marry Auntie Rae."

"Well, thank you." Even the current awkwardness couldn't suppress his smile at the irony of receiving Kristen's unsolicited permission to marry Rae when such a short time ago she had made it a point to keep him at a distance. "But Rae might have something to say about that."

"But she likes you a lot, Daniel. Auntie Rae'll marry you if you just ask her."

"Kris?" Rae's voice coming from the doorway sounded perfectly calm, but as she crossed the room to take a seat on the sofa beside Kristen, a blush crept across her cheeks. "Did I catch you playing matchmaker?"

"No, ma'am." With a guilty expression, the little girl scooted closer to Daniel. "But if you marry Daniel, he can come and live with us, that's all."

"And you'd like that?" Rae asked.

Kristen nodded. "Wouldn't you?"

Rae gave him an apologetic glance over Kristen's head. "Sweetie, it's more complicated than that. For two people to decide to get married, they have to know each other very well. They have to love each other and want to be together for always. And that takes time."

"How long?" Kristen insisted.

"Depends. Sometimes a few months, sometimes longer."

Bursting into tears, Kristen sobbed, "But that'll be too late. You have to marry Daniel *now*, so he can come and live with us and be our new daddy, so we won't have to go away."

"Oh, Kris," Rae said. An expression of utter defeat filled her eyes, and she appeared incapable of responding to her niece's distress.

Instinctively, Daniel moved to fill the void. Gathering Kristen into his arms, he held her close.

"Baby, your father's not going to take you away from Rae," he said soothingly. "He can't. That was just bragging, saying he could. Believe me, I'd never leave this house if you really needed me. But you don't, not for this. Because nobody's going to take you away from here."

Sobbing, Kristen clung to him. Exhausted by the emotionally draining events of the day, she didn't cry for very long. When her tears finally diminished to sniffles and hiccups, she mumbled, "Promise?"

"Absolutely."

"Auntie Rae," she said sleepily, "do you promise, too?"

After a long, hard look at him, Rae said, "I believe Daniel."

Deeply grateful for her demonstration of faith, he reached out to draw her to his side, and with the most recent crisis over, the three of them sat quietly until Kristen fell asleep.

"Shouldn't we get her to bed?" he whispered.

Rae nodded. Getting to her feet, she reached as if to take Kristen from him, but instead, she pulled back. "Will you bring her upstairs?"

With the child in his arms, he got up from the sofa and followed Rae to the room the two girls shared. After laying Kristen gently on her bed, he took a seat in the old-fashioned rocker positioned conveniently between the twin beds and watched Rae lovingly prepare her niece for sleep. Then, with both girls tucked in for the night, he and Rae left to return downstairs.

"I'm sorry Kristen embarrassed you," she said as they started down the stairs.

Draping his arm across her shoulders, he drew her close. "She didn't say anything that hasn't already crossed my mind a time or two."

"Marrying me to protect the girls?"

Smiling, he bent forward to give her a tender kiss before saying, "The first part."

"How could you even think about marriage when you don't trust me enough to tell me what you know about Steve's threat?"

He let out a long, slow breath as they turned in unison to continue down the stairs. Still undecided about how to handle the situation, he would have to wing it. "It's not that easy."

When they reached the bottom of the staircase, she spun around to face him. Clutching his arms above the elbows, she said, "You do know something."

He nodded, loosening her grip enough to take her into his arms. "Steve'll never be able to take the girls away from you. But don't ask how I know."

"I have to. Kris and Erin need the love and security of a proper home. It's my responsibility to make sure they have it." Stepping away from him, she sank to the stairs, taking a seat there as she gazed dejectedly up at him. "Don't you see? If you won't help me, I'll have to pay Steve off."

"Don't do it, Rae. Don't let him drag you down with him." He seated himself beside her. Grasping her shoulders, he turned her to face him. "Hold on and ride it out and let him hang himself. He can't hurt the girls. I give you my word. Can't that be enough?"

Pulling away from him, she hugged her knees to her chest, resting her head atop them as she spoke, her voice filled with pain. "I put my life in your hands once before, and I'd do it again in a heartbeat. But we're not talking about *my* life now. This concerns my nieces, and I need more than blind faith to go on."

"My word's that big a gamble?"

She looked over at him, her eyes brimming with tears. "Please don't make it a choice between you and the children," she whispered hoarsely. "I love you,

Daniel, and I believe in you, just like Kris and Erin believe in me. But they can't protect themselves in this. That's up to me. How could I live with myself if I didn't do everything possible to keep them safe? Your word's good enough for me, and that's all I'm asking for. Tell me what you know. You don't have to show proof."

"All right." With a deep sigh, he sat back against the balustrade. "It'll come out in court anyway, but if he got wind of it before then . . ."

"You think I'd tell him?"

"Not on purpose." He looked down at his hands. "This afternoon, though, you got pretty upset. What if that happened again?"

She nodded. "I see. When things get tough, you think I'll sell you out."

"Oh, Rae." Stalling, he ran a hand over his eyes. Having decided to reveal what he'd learned, he now had to find the least alarming way to do it. "It's not a matter of trust between you and me. I took an oath, and I just don't like the idea of breaking it."

"I know," she said, her gold-brown eyes filled with a mixture of urgency and regret. "Except for Steve and his threats, I'd never ask you to, but he didn't leave me much choice."

"Okay." Daniel reached for her hand, cradling it between his. "Getting ready for court, New World's attorneys ran a check on Steve, and they found some pretty ugly stuff."

"Like what?"

"He's a crook."

Registering no surprise whatsoever, she asked, "Blackmail? He's done this before?"

Daniel shook his head. "Fraud. That big, fancy automobile dealership of his hasn't made a penny in years."

"That can't be. Karen and Steve did some pretty high living. They couldn't have managed on Karen's earnings alone—not with two children to support. The studios make good money, but nowhere near what it would take to cover their expenses. He had to be bringing in a bundle.''

''Yeah, but not only from selling cars. He used that as a front while he cheated people out of a fortune.''

''How? What could he possibly have that would be worth so much?''

''He claimed to be developing a mass-producible, mass-marketable, solar-powered car. He sold Dallas as the future mecca of automotive production, bigger and better than Detroit and immune to the kind of decay that's destroying the original automobile capital. He kept his victims on the line by issuing regular, professional-looking status reports that always included the latest photographs of the 'prototype.' He took 'em for millions.''

''Then why haven't the pictures hit the press? And didn't any of his so-called investors insist on seeing the test model in person?''

''Uh-uh. He's apparently quite a con man. He convinced his marks that his 'engineers' had come up with a new design that overcame the well-known limitations of solar power. And he stressed secrecy. Couldn't take a chance on having his idea stolen, could he? The payoff must've been worth the risk of somebody turning the faked photos over to the news media. Besides, he specialized in swindling the mega-rich, like your parents. With so much spare change sitting around, maybe it wasn't worth their time to check him out more thoroughly.''

''But how long could he hope to get away with it? Eventually, even the petty-cash box gets audited.''

''He won't deal with accountants and the like. He does business directly with the investors, and he's managed to keep it rolling for years. His big mistake was filing suit against New World. When our investigators

took their evidence to the authorities, they started their
own investigation. I hoped they'd indict him before the
suit went to trial, but in any case, he'll probably go to
prison. If he does, it shouldn't be a problem for you
to get permanent custody of the girls.''

The tears he'd watched her struggling against all day
long coursed down her cheeks. Pulling her to him, he
held her in a tight embrace until her tears of relief
subsided.

When she could speak again, she said, ''With all that
money coming in, why'd he bother to blackmail me?''

''He got careless, and the funds are beginning to dry
up. Meanwhile, he's in hock up to the hilt. He's even
started milking the car dealership, after using it for so
long as a front. They're getting complaints from people
who traded in used cars on new ones, then found out
the loans on the old cars never got paid off. The dealership's also been accused of taking tax, title, and license
money without providing the services. The empire he
built upon the sand has started to sink.''

''And in desperation, he decided to put the bite on
me.''

Daniel nodded. ''But don't even think about giving
him money—or anything else that could be converted
into quick cash. You haven't, have you, Rae?''

She shook her head, bewilderment in her eyes. ''Not
that I remember. What's the problem?''

''Rae, he's your brother-in-law, his wife was your
sister and partner, and you're raising his kids. On the
surface, that looks like a pretty close relationship. Any
money changing hands, for whatever reason, could implicate you in his racket.''

──────── THIRTEEN ────────

Dumbfounded, Rae stared at Daniel. Just when she had begun to hope her troubles were over, he presented her with this new, more ominous possibility.

Finding her voice at last, she said, "I don't know how much more of this I can take. It's like a nightmare I can't wake up from."

"Steer clear of Steve, and it'll be okay," Daniel said soothingly, the depth of his concern clearly written in his expression. "But think again, Rae. Have you ever given him anything—anything at all—that somebody might think was front money?"

Like the proverbial drowning man, she mentally ran through her entire adult life in a matter of minutes. Approaching the present, she shook her head. "Nothing . . . well . . . except for Christmases and birthdays. Just token stuff. Not money. Cash gifts aren't in very good taste." Well, that did it. She had surely lost her mind this time. Instructing someone in proper etiquette, with her whole life crumbling around her, definitely wasn't a sign of good mental health.

Daniel smiled. "Then we'll be all right."

She nodded, unable to share the relief shining in

Daniel's eyes. For her, the details, like the pieces of some gigantic jigsaw puzzle, wouldn't fit together. Frustrated by the nagging uncertainties that continued to nibble at the edges of her mind, she said, as much to herself as to him, "How could Steve pull off something like that right under my nose? And what about Karen? How'd he hide it from her?"

"Don't know." He looked away from her, and his optimism, so apparent only moments earlier, evaporated. "But you're not the only one asking those questions."

She covered her face with her hands, once again ready to give in to tears. "And how am I supposed to answer? That he fooled us, too, and I'm as much in the dark as everybody else? It's not possible. He couldn't have done it."

"You don't think he's capable of fraud?"

Raising her head, she looked into a pair of distinctly skeptical smoky gray eyes. "Don't get me wrong. It's not character I'm talking about. It's intelligence. He's just not smart enough to come up with a plot like that, much less make it work. He's got to be working for somebody else."

With an almost reflexive reaction, he turned away to gaze at the floor, but he said nothing.

Exhausted, she leaned back against the wall. "Who is it, Daniel?"

Remaining silent, he shrugged as if to ask what she meant.

"The accomplice you forgot to tell me about," she said tiredly. "Who is it?"

"Rae," he said, revealing fatigue that matched her own, "I've already broken my word not to talk about this, and I told you enough so you don't have to worry about losing the girls. Please, don't ask for more."

His words knifed through her, and she hugged her arms to her stomach as she tried to ignore the guilt she felt at her part in the breaking of his pledge. For him, a betrayal of trust was no small matter. It would haunt him for a long time, and it could well alter his feelings for her. Her concern for her nieces, however, overrode her distress at having to press him further.

"Daniel, I'll never forget this, and even though you might not believe it, I know how hard it's been for you."

He sighed deeply. "But?"

"But . . . if I could end up in jail right along with Steve, then who'd take care of Kristen and Erin?" She turned away, no longer able to bear the effect her questions were having on him as his entire body tensed. "What if they think I'm the one working with him? I wouldn't put it past him to implicate me out of spite. And as much as that scares me, it's even worse to think of my nieces growing up in boarding schools and summer camps like Karen and I did."

"That won't happen."

"It could if the authorities can't identify Steve's partner."

"They have." He gripped her shoulders as he turned her to him and looked deeply into her eyes. "God, Rae, I didn't want to be the one to tell you. You'll have to know sometime, though, and I guess it's better to hear it from me than anyone else." He took a deep breath. "Yes, Steve had an accomplice who thought of the scheme, developed it, and fine-tuned it through the years. You're right. Steve's not smart enough for that. He contributed charm and the ability to sell sirloin to vegetarians. They made quite a team."

"Made? The partnership's over?"

He nodded. "Steve's been on his own for a couple of years. That's why it's falling apart on him."

"Who?" she whispered, her heart racing in anticipation.

Looking past her, he gazed into space as if struggling through some private hell, and when he reached to draw her into his arms, he closed his eyes against the secret knowledge he had yet to share with her. For a few minutes, he held her so tightly that she could feel every muscle in his body tensed as though for battle until, at last, he said hoarsely, "It was Karen."

It took a few seconds for the words to reach Rae's brain and a bit longer for her to comprehend their meaning. When their significance dawned, however, she tore herself from his embrace. Leaping to her feet, she stared down at him, searching for proof that this man was the same person she had fallen in love with. Everything seemed unchanged—his dark, gray-flecked hair, deep gray eyes, the mouth that could turn her knees to jelly just by curving up at one corner, and strong, graceful hands that excited her in ways no one else's ever could. But some creature must have appropriated his body for its own use, because the Daniel she loved could never say anything so vile about her sister.

"It's some kind of joke!" The hoarse croak that issued from her throat startled her with its harsh sound.

"No," he said soothingly. "I wouldn't do that to you."

"Then you've lost your mind."

With undeniable sadness, he shook his head. "I've seen the evidence."

The gentleness in his voice contrasted sharply with the stridency of hers. Still, she found it impossible to moderate her tone.

"My sister a criminal? Impossible. She couldn't do that. And she never kept secrets from me."

"She did, Rae. A lot of them."

"You're wrong. You don't understand how close we were. We shared everything." Rae shook her head, nearly overpowered by the urge to laugh at such absurdity. "Oh, she could be wild and impulsive at times, but she could never, never have done what you say she did. Even if she had, she couldn't have kept it hidden from me."

"Don't say that when you're questioned. They might take you at your word."

"Frankly, your concern's a little hard to swallow under the circumstances."

"Rae, listen carefully." He reached up to take her hands into his.

Sickened by his disloyalty, she jerked free of him, provoking a flash of emotion in his eyes that she once would have interpreted as pain.

Looking down at the floor, he crossed his arms across his chest. "I see," he said quietly. "Rae, try to understand. How can I get through to you?"

"Her motive. If she was the mastermind, tell me what made her do it. Not money. She'd already disposed of more than she could have swindled out of anybody. So tell me, Daniel, what turned my sister into a criminal?"

"How do I know? I never met her."

"No, but that hasn't stopped you from trying to ruin her reputation."

"Oh, Rae." It came out almost a groan. "You can't believe that. Why would I want to bad-mouth your sister?"

"To cover your own mistakes? Maybe you're not as innocent as you want everyone to think." The words formed a band that coiled itself around her heart, squeezing tighter and tighter with excruciating precision to smother the last trace of compassion still harbored there. "Maybe you're more frightened of that trial than you pretend to be, and maybe, just maybe, the only thing Steve got right was the reason you got involved with me."

His face paled, but he said nothing.

Barely pausing for breath, she went on. "Good old Steve said you'd do anything to improve your chances in court, and it's true. Nothing's out of bounds to you—not even attacking the reputation of a woman who can't defend herself and romancing her sister.''

Drained both emotionally and physically, Rae felt herself begin to wilt as she fought to keep her knees from buckling beneath her. Daniel, however, didn't move a muscle or utter a sound. A man falsely accused would defend himself against such charges. Though she waited, giving him ample opportunity to counter her assertions, he raised not one objection. Her last glimmer of hope died in his silence, leaving her groping in the dark of a vast, aching emptiness.

''I have to hand it to you. You were convincing.'' Unable to muster the sarcasm she aimed for, she sounded more like a heartbroken child than a woman avenging a grievous wrong. ''I believed you when you said you loved me. What a brilliant liar. You fooled me completely. With that kind of talent, it probably wasn't too hard to mislead the NTSB about the plane crash.

''What really happened in the cockpit that day, Captain MacKay? Were your decisions so flawed that the only way you can live with yourself is to cheapen the lives of the passengers you killed? Well, you'd better find another way. I won't let you victimize Karen a second time.''

Daniel stood up and stared into Rae's eyes for a long moment. Then, without disturbing the heavy silence that settled between them, he turned to walk out of her home. And out of her life.

''Don't wanna go to Elena's, Auntie Rae,'' Erin whined, squirming to avoid having her hair brushed. ''Wanna stay home with you.''

Setting the child firmly in her chair, Rae snapped, ''Be still, we're running late.''

Pouting, Erin fell silent, but she made no attempt to

hide her unhappiness from her aunt as she glared into the mirror.

"Besides," Rae continued, her tone moderating as her irritation subsided, "I won't be here today. That's why you're staying with Elena and Manny for a while, remember? There, now, that wasn't so bad, was it?" Giving Erin's unruly red curls one last pat, she helped the little girl down before Kristen climbed into the vacated chair.

Kristen sat absolutely still, watching Rae's every move reflected in the mirror as she began combing the child's hair into place.

Rae managed to muster a smile for her nieces. "Don't you like visiting Elena's family?"

"Mostly," Kristen answered quietly. "But this is different."

"Maybe for a little longer, that's all." Rae reached for a barrette and fastened Kristen's hair back out of her face. "Depends on when they call me to the witness stand. I might be tied up a couple of days, and by that time Elena and Manny will have you so spoiled you won't want to come home. You'll see." Finished with the child's hair, she helped her down from the chair. "Wait for me downstairs, but remember, don't go outside. I'll be down in a couple of seconds."

The girls left, allowing Rae to concentrate on her own hair.

Lately, her nieces had stopped asking why they could no longer play outdoors unless she or Elena was with them. They adapted quickly to the new rules imposed on them in the past month. A month? It seemed like a year since Steve had issued the ultimatum that had affected every aspect of her life. She couldn't even remember the last time she'd had a sound night's sleep. Except for provoking those sleepless nights and the need to maintain constant watch over the children, however, Steve had caused little trouble. He'd called a number of times, but she'd had no trouble dealing with his nuisance telephone calls, and only once had he summoned the nerve to show up in person. After having the Decatur police remove him from her front porch, Rae had expected an angry reaction. Instead, he'd remained unusually quiet. Still, she had thought it best to keep up her guard. No telling what he might do when freed from the distraction of the civil trial.

The trial! If she didn't get moving, Dallas County would be sending their deputies for her. With a hasty last glance in the mirror, she headed for the stairs. As she started down, however, Erin's voice, floating up from the front hall, stopped her.

". . . hurted my feelings."

"I know," Kristen said with a deep sigh. "It's 'cause she's sad."

" 'Bout what?"

" 'Cause Mr. Daniel went away."

"Why?"

Kristen's voice dropped almost to a whisper. "I guess he just doesn't love us enough."

Kristen's perceptive conclusion stabbed through Rae. The last thing she wanted was for Kris and Erin to feel responsible for Daniel's sudden exit. Continuing down the stairs, she found her nieces waiting impatiently for her.

Bending to give them a hug, Rae said, "We need to have a little talk."

"But we're late, Auntie Rae," Kristen argued, looking at her aunt as if she had lost her mind. "You said so."

"I know. This is more important, though. Now, both of you listen." She paused until she had their full attention. "It's about Daniel and me. I tried to explain why we stopped seeing each other, but I guess I didn't do too good a job of it, so let's try again. Okay?"

Both girls nodded.

She took a deep breath, trying to find a fresh approach. "Well, sometimes grown-ups have a hard time getting along with each other. The last time he was here, Daniel and I had a big argument. We couldn't settle it, so we decided it would be best for us to stay away from each other. It didn't have anything to do with you girls. In fact, he enjoyed your company very much. I'm sorry we hurt you by breaking off our friendship, but letting it go on when we both knew it would never work out would have hurt us all even more."

"Did Daniel get his feelings hurt?" Kristen asked.

Taken off guard, Rae hesitated a moment before answering. "I don't . . . well, maybe."

"You did," Kristen said softly. "I don't like it when you're sad."

"Everybody wants the people they love to be happy. But every now and then we all get a little blue. We just can't help it." Again she hugged the girls tightly. "Sorry about being extra grouchy lately. I'll try to do better."

Kris nodded. "And we'll try to be real good." When Erin didn't speak, Kristen gave her sister a little shove. "Huh, Eri?"

"Okeydoke." Erin pulled away from Rae. "Let's go."

While neither child complained again about having to stay at Elena's for a day or two, neither did they seem happy about it as Rae drove away after dropping them off. Her nieces' low spirits would rebound quickly, though. Among Elena's large, friendly family, they would soon forget their troubles. Her own day would have no such happy ending.

Subpoenaed by Steve's attorney, she had no choice but to turn her truck toward the place she least wished to be. Facing both Steve and Daniel across a courtroom while she recounted the details of Karen's life and death would challenge her control to the limit. With Daniel's support, it would have been difficult enough. As things stood, getting through it without having an emotional breakdown was the best she could hope for.

Arriving at her destination, she parked, paid the attendant, and walked slowly toward the courthouse, her apprehension growing as she neared the building. Just going through the door took all her courage. How would she ever make it upstairs to the courtroom? Pausing in the lobby, she looked around to get her bearings as she fought the temptation to run away from the ordeal awaiting her.

"Rae?"

At the sound of Jenna's voice, relief flooded through her. Spinning around to face her friend, Rae said, "You're the last person I expected to see here this morning, but you couldn't have picked a better time to show up. One second later, and you'd have caught me running out the door."

With a sympathetic hug, Jenna said, "We thought you might need a friendly face, even if it's only for a minute, so we came over before work."

"We? Who'd you bring with you?" Rae looked around for anyone else she might recognize.

"Just Eddie," Jenna said quickly. "He gave me a ride." She linked arms with a darkly handsome man who stood casually aside, turned partially away from them. Drawing him nearer to her and Rae, she said, "I know it's a bad time . . . but . . . well . . . Rae, this is Eddie Montoya—you know, from childbirth class."

Extending her hand, Rae looked into the young man's familiar black eyes. "Eduardo? Good to see you again, but it's been so long, I'm not sure I'd have recognized you if Jenna hadn't told me your name."

"Miss Garrett?" the young man responded, looking surprised.

"Well," Jenna said with a shrug. "Small-world syndrome. You know each other?"

"Sure," Rae answered. "I've met all of Elena's children." She paused, putting this new information together with everything else Jenna had told her about the persistent young man from childbirth class. "Oh, I see. It was Marisela. You mistook his sister for his wife."

Eddie nodded. "Sela's husband passed out when their first baby was born. That's why I'm standing in this time." He grinned. "I couldn't understand why Jenna avoided me like the plague until she agreed to come to dinner at my home a couple of weeks ago. That's when we got it all straightened out."

Jenna nodded. "His whole family got a laugh out of that one."

"I can imagine," Rae said, unable to summon the smile she tried for. "But at the Montoyas, you must have recognized Elena."

"How?" Jenna asked. "The few times I made it out to your place, she'd already left, and when I finally did meet her, everybody called her Mama. I don't have the slightest idea how we missed all the other signals."

"We'll figure it out later," Eddie said.

Jenna gave Rae an encouraging pat on the arm. "I was waiting for the right time to tell you about this, and now I've managed to pick the worst time of all."

"Your timing's great," Rae said. "It's good to see somebody smiling for a change, especially somebody who means as much to me as you do." She glanced at her watch. "Almost time. I should already be upstairs."

Jenna gave her another comforting hug. "Wish I could stay."

Rae returned her friend's hug before stepping away. "Take care of things at the studio. That's where I need you most. But thanks for coming this morning." She turned toward Eddie. "Thank you both."

Eddie shook her extended hand. "I hope it turns out okay."

This time, Rae managed a smile. "I'll get through it. Good friends and good wishes help more than you know."

After walking Rae to the elevator, Eddie and Jenna left. Alone, once again Rae fought pervasive dread. On the witness stand she would give her view of what happened the day of the accident. Beyond that, she could only describe the effect Karen's death had on her and the children. But how deeply would they probe into the details of Karen's life? Would the attorneys ask intimate questions she might not feel comfortable answering in public?

Stepping off the elevator, Rae checked in with the representative for Steve's attorney, received instructions from court officials, and settled in to wait for the bailiff to call her to the stand. With her nerves stretched tight, every movement in the bustling hall caused a moment's panic and every sound grated like fingernails on a blackboard, stretching each passing second into endless agony. By the lunchtime adjournment, she still hadn't been called, and, afraid she would be unable to force herself to return to the courthouse, she settled for a cup of tea in the basement cafeteria. When court reconvened, she was summoned immediately.

Following the bailiff, she kept her eyes on the floor to avoid any exchange whatsoever with either Steve or Daniel as she made her way down the aisle. Pausing, she waited for the bailiff to open the gate that separated spectators and members of the press from those involved in the court proceedings, and as she walked through it, she discovered herself facing the judicial bench and the jury box across an expanse of gray linoleum-covered floor. Courage deserted her. If not for the numerous pairs of eyes boring into her back, she would have bolted for the door. Instead, she clenched her hands to stop them from shaking and willed her legs to support her until she somehow managed to cross to the witness stand.

Rae could feel the stares as she raised her hand to take the oath required of all witnesses. The words of the rapidly intoned pledge ran together in an incomprehensible stream, their meaning lost in her anxiety, but she would have sworn to anything to get the ordeal over with. Hoping her promise required no more of her than to tell the truth, she managed a muted "I do."

She took the steps to the witness stand carefully, her knees threatening to fold up on her at each new level. She had no intention, however, of falling flat on her face as a prelude to her testimony. Her words alone would have to satisfy the curiosity seekers.

At last she settled into the chair provided. Facing a roomful of strangers, she kept her eyes glued on the floor, unwilling to risk an inadvertent encounter with either of her betrayers. Evading their probing eyes proved more difficult. She could feel Daniel's intense gaze fixed on her, and she shrank from the sensation of intimacy it provoked as she began answering the questions posed by Steve's attorney. In a voice so soft she had to be reminded several times to speak up, she recounted her sister's life as the lawyer purposefully guided her through her statement.

Memories of Karen more vivid than any Rae had experienced in months came back to haunt her as she related details of the beautiful, vivacious woman, the warm, loving mother, the astute business partner she had known her sister to be. Missing her more than at any time since she'd first learned of Karen's death, Rae had to pause frequently to regain control over the tears that threatened to turn her into an incoherent, babbling mass.

Grateful when the painful inquisition ended without her falling apart completely, she rose to leave. The judge, however, stopped her with a reminder of the defendants' right of cross-examination, and steeling herself against further intrusion into Karen's life, she sat back down.

"Thank you very much, Miss Garrett, for favoring us with a little more of your valuable time," one of the airline's attorneys said, eliciting chuckles from the spectators.

He paused, and Rae could hear his footsteps approaching. When he stopped directly in front of the witness stand, she couldn't help taking note of the large, heavyset man wearing a dark, wrinkled suit, his brightly colored paisley tie askew. Leaning forward until his face was mere inches from hers, he gave a predatory smile that made her blood run cold.

"Tell me, Miss Garrett," he said, his voice dripping with sarcasm, "just how deeply involved were you in that cozy little setup your sainted sister ran with the assistance of that angelic husband of hers?"

FOURTEEN

For the first time since she had taken the stand, Rae looked up. Turning to stare directly at Daniel, she felt a stab of disappointment as sharp and as fresh as when she first understood that she was nothing more to him than the means to a self-serving end. Tears clouded her vision, but she quickly swallowed them. She refused to let anyone see that the hypocrite she had once viewed as a hero could still make her want to believe in his declarations of love. Denying its existence, however, didn't eliminate the attraction that extended even across an impersonal courtroom to heighten the pain of his betrayal.

At least he hadn't let her walk unprepared into the trap set by New World Airways' attorneys. He'd warned her that they intended to use the alleged fraud scheme to discredit Karen. Unfortunately, his twinge of conscience hadn't extended to helping prevent the scurrilous attack on her sister's character, and the question posed by the lawyer acting on his behalf exposed the current proceeding's illusion of fairness, decency, and honor for what it was—a well-played farce.

Returning her gaze, Daniel didn't even look ashamed of being a party to slander.

"Did you hear the question, Miss Garrett?" the attorney said derisively. "Or don't you plan to honor us with your comments today?"

Readjusting her attention to focus on the man standing in front of her, she found herself transfixed by a stray tuft of gray hair that had sprung loose from the carefully combed locks covering his receding hairline. Watching it bounce straight up with each word he spoke gave her a strange sense of composure. She would let no one, especially this unkempt buffoon, smear her sister's reputation.

Drawing herself up tall in her chair, she lifted her chin as she faced the hired character assassin who confronted her. "What kind of answer do you expect to that sort of nonsense?"

He grinned. "An honest one. I notice you didn't have to ask what I meant. But then, you'd already be familiar with the details, wouldn't you?"

"I know what you're talking about," Rae answered, refusing to be intimidated by his imperious manner. "Somebody warned me you'd be spreading lies about my sister."

He lost his self-satisfied grin, his eyes narrowing with skepticism as he pursed his lips. "Is that so?" Leaning on the rail bordering the witness stand, he turned half-way around, gesturing toward Steve. "I can't believe your—let's just call him your brother-in-law—would have shown up today if he had any idea we were onto him. So would you care to tell the court who the source of your information is?"

Again she stared at Daniel. By participating in this kangaroo court, he invalidated everything that had ever passed between them. Under the circumstances, she felt no obligation to protect his confidentiality. Only personal honor kept her from naming him. "No," she said quietly, "I would not."

Following her gaze, the interrogator kept his back to her as he said, "I could ask the judge to instruct you to answer. If he did and you still refused, you could be held in contempt." He turned to face her. "You could go to jail, Miss Garrett. Would you be willing to go to jail to keep your secret?"

At the suggestion of her imprisonment, she felt the blood drain from her face, and moisture drenched her palms as she clasped her hands tightly together. Daniel, looking intently at her, moved his head slightly from side to side. But she needed no reminder of her pledge not to expose his double-dealing. Unlike others in the courtroom, she would keep her word. "I would," she whispered. Instructed to speak up, she said loudly, "Yes."

Closing his eyes, Daniel dropped his head forward to rest his face in his hands. Relief, she supposed. He wouldn't care that covering for him might land her in jail. Horrified by the prospect, she gritted her teeth, and every muscle in her body tensed as she waited for the cross-examiner's next move.

Again the oversized lawyer turned around to look in Daniel's direction. After a long, tortuous pause he finally said, "Fortunately for you, Miss Garrett, I won't demand an answer—this time. Now, let's stop tap-dancing around the issue and get down to brass tacks. Who picked the pigeons, you or your sister?"

As the realization set in that she wouldn't, for the present, be imprisoned, her poise returned. Gazing steadily into the eyes of her inquisitor, she joined the fray, armed with absolute confidence in her sister's integrity.

For the rest of the afternoon, she sparred with the airline's representative. He made accusation after accusation against Karen and Steve, often over the objection of Steve's attorney. The supporting evidence he presented, however, while clearly implicating Steve, proved nothing against her sister, and Rae managed to rebut many of the references to Karen's involvement. At the end of the day, her faith in Karen remained intact.

Returning for her second day of testimony was one of the most difficult things she had ever been required to do. Nothing less than defending Karen's honor would have made it worthwhile as, once again summoning courage she never knew she possessed, she took the witness stand.

She had half expected to arrive in court to discover Steve had absconded during the night, leaving her holding the bag for his criminal behavior. His appearance at the plaintiff's table provided her first surprise of the day. The second began with a flurry of activity at the courtroom door. When the excitement abated, she was stunned to see Nick and Edie stride up the center aisle to take seats in the front row.

That was all she needed. With the news media already in a frenzy over the latest developments in this case, her parents' appearance would only inspire them to greater heights of tasteless intrusion. Protecting Kristen and Erin from the sensationalism would now be all but impossible. It wouldn't take an overzealous professional snoop long to find them at Elena's.

Preoccupied by this new worry, Rae blanched when the judge gaveled for order. She had barely recovered before the same officious attorney she'd squared off with the previous day began a new round of interrogation.

The moment he posed his first question, Rae understood that yesterday's grilling had been a picnic compared to what she would face today. Clearly he had saved his big guns for a decisive conclusion.

Systematically, he laid out his case. Probing and prodding, he chided her when she repeatedly answered, "I don't know," to his increasingly hostile demands for explanations she had no way of providing. On several occasions he bullied her nearly to tears, implying with his scornful smirk, when she needed time to compose herself, that her reactions were a carefully rehearsed performance rather than genuine emotion. As soon as she recovered, he attacked again.

The amount and quality of the corroborating evidence he presented in support of his allegations disturbed Rae more than the incessant verbal assault. The harangue she could tolerate. Accepting the data linking Karen to the fraud proved much more unsettling. Confused, she studied each successive exhibit carefully, seeking some bit of overlooked information that would absolve her sister. She found none. Instead, the documents—some in a computer code that bore characteristics of Karen's methodology and some in Karen's own handwriting— painted a picture of a woman Rae had never known at all.

By the time she was dismissed from the witness stand at the end of the day, she could no longer deny that Karen had indeed participated substantially in the massive swindle. Deeply wounded by her sister's betrayal, Rae fled the courtroom, pushing her way through a crush of merciless reporters. As she reached the elevators, her parents caught up with her.

"Darling," Edie said. "Slow down. Your father and I wish to speak with you."

"Do you really?" Rae replied coolly, taking refuge deep within herself. "About what?"

Nick moved to shield her from reporters as much as possible. "Rae, you should have told us about this. We learned of it on television. You can't imagine our shock."

"But you weren't so stunned that you couldn't rush right to the center of the media spotlight," Rae answered, unable to disguise the sarcasm in her voice. "What for? Hoping to turn the news coverage into an appeal for funds for Ease Human Suffering? Or did your beloved son-in-law convince you to spread some of your money around to keep him out of prison? If you came to gloat, then I guess you're entitled to. You were right about Karen all along."

Edie grasped Rae's shoulders, looking her straight in the eye. "My dear, we know well enough what you think of us as parents. Perhaps we earned your opinion. Regardless of our mistakes, though, we do care for you. Knowing how you idolized your sister, we couldn't help but worry about how this would affect you. We thought you might need . . . someone."

The elevator doors opened. Rae entered, turning to look at her parents, who could not force their way into the crowded car. Utterly disconnected from the rest of the world, she couldn't even summon the usual dislike as she returned her mother's gaze. With a frigid lack of emotion, she answered, "Well, you were wrong. I don't need anybody."

The moment the gavel sounded, signaling the end of the current court session, Daniel ran after Rae. Her expression as she left the courtroom sent chills running up and down his spine. In the time he'd known her, he'd seen her angry; he'd seen her scared; he'd seen her aflame with passion. He had never looked into her eyes and found them devoid of any feeling whatsoever. Her dispirited demeanor scared him senseless.

Elbowing his way through the crowd of gossipmongers, he rounded the corner to the bank of elevators in time to see her step into one. Maneuvering close enough to overhear her departing words to her parents, he was struck once again by her detached manner, and the iciness of her tone stopped him in his tracks. When he recovered, the doors had closed, and the elevator had begun its descent.

Disregarding the usual formalities, he approached

Nick and Edie. "Rae had the rug pulled out from under her in the courtroom today, and she looked pretty upset to me. How did she seem to you?"

"She's in great pain, Mr. MacKay," Edie answered with a catch in her voice. "Right now, she needs someone she can trust. I'm afraid Nick and I don't qualify for that."

"I'm not sure I do, either," Daniel admitted unhappily. "You must've noticed we weren't exactly on the same side back there, and if you ask me, it'll be a long time before Rae believes in anyone again."

"Perhaps," Nick said with a sigh. "But loyalty is my daughter's strength as well as her weakness. You were close to her once. I know the trust you shared remains with her, no matter what's happened between you since. You may be the only one who can show her that she hasn't been abandoned." His voice dropped to a whisper. "Again."

Hope sent renewed energy coursing through Daniel. "Rae say where she's headed?"

They shook their heads.

Her eyes brimming with tears, Edie said, "You know her friends and her habits. You have a better chance of finding our daughter than we do. Please try, Mr. MacKay. She's in such pain—" She choked, and her voice dwindled off.

"I'll do my best." Wasting no more time, Daniel sprinted for the stairs. Tackling them at top speed, he ran down the seven flights to the lobby, not slowing until he reached the parking lot. He arrived in time to see Rae's truck disappear into the rush-hour traffic. Gulping air into his lungs, he took a few minutes to catch his breath before heading to his own car.

He slid in behind the wheel. He would check with Elena first. Even after a battering like the one she had taken in court, Rae would want to see the children. Pulling into the street, he headed for Decatur.

But Rae wasn't at Elena's. Neither was she with Jenna, nor at the studio. No one had heard from her. Once again he went over his mental list of Rae's friends, hoping to come up with an idea he'd over-looked earlier. None occurred to him. He had already checked everywhere she might have sought consolation, even Black Creek Lake.

Returning to town, he located a public telephone in front of a convenience store not far from Rae's home. However, the hours he spent dialing number after number and the mounds of quarters he invested in calls to hospitals and police agencies all over north Texas yielded nothing.

Out of clues, he headed once more for Rae's. Although he held out little hope that she had returned home since the last time he'd driven by, he felt compelled to give it another try before he started back to his own apartment. At last his effort paid off. Her truck was parked in the drive.

Relief flooded through him, and enormous tension instantly exited his body, leaving him momentarily light-headed. He slammed on his brakes. As soon as the car came to a stop, he jumped out, brushing past the lone reporter still dogging Rae. Hurrying up the walk, he felt better about the world than he had in weeks until he bounded up the porch steps to discover the front door standing wide open. At well past midnight, it should have been shut, locked, and bolted. His newfound optimism faded.

Stepping into the unlit hall, he closed the door behind him. No light shone anywhere in the house. "Rae," he called, blinking in the unfamiliar darkness. "It's me."

No answer.

Switching on a light, he walked further into the hall and tried again. "Rae, where are you?"

Silence.

Okay, he'd search the whole house, top to bottom, if he had to. Whatever her reasons for not wanting to see him, he couldn't honor them until he saw for himself that she was all right.

She had probably headed straight for bed the moment she arrived home, making her bedroom the logical place for him to start looking. On his way toward the staircase, however, he noticed the living room door ajar. His heart skipped a beat as he slowly pushed it open. "Rae?"

The shaft of light from the open door fell across the sofa, dimly illuminating her motionless form as she sat in the dark staring up at her sister's portrait. Pain radiated from her, hitting him with an almost physical force that momentarily robbed him of breath as he crossed the room to take a seat beside her.

"Everybody's been worried about you," he said, trying to keep his voice as normal-sounding as possible while he fought the urge to take her in his arms. "When you disappeared like that after court . . . well, we were worried." He paused. When she said nothing, he continued. "Finding your front door open gave me a jolt, too. Anybody could have walked in on you—some weirdo or even that reporter hanging around outside."

She still didn't respond, leaving him groping for a way to reach her. If her wound were physical, he would have some idea how to treat it, but this intense psychic pain was outside the realm of his experience. For this he had nothing to offer other than his presence. He would stay with her until she asked him to leave.

With her head resting on the back of the sofa, she continued to gaze at the picture. Profound grief distorted her features, making him ache to take her in his arms, to hold her, rock her, whisper the words that could give her comfort the way he had once seen her soothe her nieces. But he didn't know the words that could bridge the distance she now used as a protective shield. Incapable of relieving her distress, he felt totally useless.

When he could no longer bear her stark expression, he followed her gaze to the portrait. Lit by the moonlight streaming in from the window, the eyes sparkled, making the hauntingly beautiful woman looking down at them seem almost lifelike. The effect wouldn't be lost on Rae as she sat, silent and absolutely still, transfixed by her sister's likeness. He could only guess what it did to her inside.

An eternity passed before her whisper broke the silence. "I adored her," she said, not moving a muscle except to speak. "Karen. My mentor, my ideal—so perfect that I modeled my whole life after her." She paused before adding plaintively, "I thought she loved me, too."

A tear trickled down her cheek, dismantling the emotional fortress she had erected around herself, and at last Daniel felt free to reach out to her. Placing his hand over hers where it it lay on the sofa, ice-cold even in the Texas heat, he said softly, "Karen did love you. A lot."

"God, I was a fool." A touch of bitterness entered Rae's voice. "To her, the whole thing was probably just a game. An amusement. And as usual, I'm the one left to face the consequences. Me and her daughters. She didn't even think of them. If that was her idea of love, we could've done with a little less of it."

He took her hand between his, rubbing gently to restore its warmth. "But Karen didn't mean for it to end up like this. Think how hard she must've worked to keep you from finding out. As close as you were, working side by side, it couldn't have been easy, but she kept her secret because your love and respect were important to her. And she didn't know she was going to die. She never got the chance to explain or to tie up loose ends. I'll bet she would've found a way to keep you and the girls out of it if she'd had the chance. When it came right down to it, Rae, she chose you, not Steve, to take care of her daughters. That says a lot about who she really trusted."

"Oh, Karen." Her words came out a low moan, and she broke into heart-rending sobs that vibrated throughout her body as she mourned the second loss of her sister.

Daniel gathered her into his arms. Holding her close as she wept uncontrollably, he murmured phrases he hoped might give her comfort, and while her anguish threatened to destroy his composure as well, he didn't try to halt the flow of her tears. Rae needed to cry out her grief. Taking this first painful step toward recovery would prove essential to her future well-being, and he waited patiently for the healing process to take its natural course. After a long, long time, her sobs finally began to subside, slowly tapering off to uneven gasps accompanied by a steady but diminishing stream of tears.

Gradually, she began to regain command of her emotions, but she didn't move from his embrace as she finally managed to speak. "Daniel, thank you. I really needed . . . somebody tonight," she said, fitting her words in between short, irregular breaths. "But I'm all right now. You don't have to stay."

He smoothed her hair away from her face, hooking it gently behind her ear. "Throwing me out?"

"No," she said, looking up at him. "Why would you bother about me, though?"

"Concern, I guess. Or whatever you want to call it," he said, gazing into her still-damp eyes. "I wanted to make sure you were okay, that's all."

Directing her eyes away from his, she focused on a spot somewhere near the middle of his chest. "After what I said to you . . . last time?"

He took a deep breath. "That was tough. Nothing I

hadn't heard before, but from you, well, I never saw it coming.''

She squeezed her eyes tightly shut, distress etched plainly on her features. "I'm sorry, Daniel. That's not enough, I know. Not for what I did to you. But you told me my sister was a criminal. Accepting that would have meant turning my back on my whole life.''

"Believe me, Rae, I didn't want to be the one to tell you about Karen. You didn't leave me much choice, though, and I didn't want you to get blindsided in court. I expected a strong reaction. I understood it. But, God, it hurt.''

"That's why I said it.'' Her voice dropped to a whisper. "I never believed you caused the accident, not for an instant. I just wanted to make the whole thing as painful for you as it was for me. As soon as the words left my mouth, I regretted them, and I've never been more ashamed of anything in my life.''

Swallowing the lump that had formed in his throat, he said softly, "I needed to hear you say that.''

At last she looked up, tears still clinging to her lashes as she met his gaze. "I made the wrong choice. I'd ask you to forgive me, but I've lost the right to ask you for anything.''

"Go ahead, Rae,'' he murmured. "Ask. See how fast you get what you want.''

Exhaling sharply, she slipped her arms around him, holding tight to him and burying her face in his shoulder. "You're the one I could've counted on all along,'' she said, her voice heavy with the second round of tears. "If I'd seen that sooner, maybe I'd have made different choices.''

"No. You'd do the same thing you did the first time—defend your sister like a tiger. That's the way you are, Rae. You fight for the people you love. And me, well, I'm glad we don't have to go through that again,'' he said, reaching for his handkerchief to wipe away her tears. "Future'll be a big enough challenge. Radio's reporting criminal charges were filed against Steve today. That means they'll start prying into your life pretty soon. Everything, business and personal, will be fair game."

She went limp in his arms. "Oh, God, Daniel, what'll I do?" she asked, fatigue and despair evident in her tone.

"Don't worry. We'll get you the best lawyers we can find," he said soothingly, "but first I want you to pack some stuff for you and the girls. I'm going to take you down to my parents' farm for a few days of peace and quiet before things really get hot. We can pick up Kris and Erin on the way."

"Do your parents know about this?" she asked, strength already beginning to return to her voice. "They might not like having three people they've never so much as set eyes on dumped in their laps in the middle of the night. And you need to make sure they know what they'd be letting themselves in for if some reporter happened to find us there."

He smiled, not at all surprised that her regard for others overrode her fears for herself. "I'll give 'em a call right now. They won't mind, though. Mom and Dad have been wanting to meet you, and when they find out you're bringing Kris and Erin, they'll be in hog heaven. Ever since my brother and his family moved to Minnesota, they've missed their grandchildren like crazy. Trust me." His heart stopped when he heard those two words leave his mouth. He had just asked for the one thing she wouldn't yet be prepared to give.

She studied him carefully for a few minutes, then nodded her agreement. "If it's okay with your parents, I'd like to get away for a while, but promise you won't pressure them into it."

"Won't have to," he assured her, relieved that she

had overlooked his gaffe. "Why don't you go on up and pack while I'm phoning?"

When he stood up and extended his hand to her, she took it without hesitation. Pulling her up beside him, he drew her into a warm, gentle hug. "While I'm making calls, I should probably let Nick and Edie know you're all right," he said, gingerly testing her reaction to the mention of her parents. "Okay?"

She shuddered. "I can't talk to them, Daniel. Not yet."

"You don't have to," he said comfortingly. "They've been pretty upset, though, and it didn't look like an act to me. I wouldn't feel right about letting them keep on worrying."

"You're right," she said softly, resting her forehead against his chest. "I wasn't thinking about them. They must have been shocked to find out about Karen, too."

"I suppose, but I think they're more concerned about you." He hesitated briefly. "Nick and Edie plan to stay in town for a while. Can I tell them you'll call when you've had a chance to rest?"

For several minutes she remained silent. Then she drew a deep breath and whispered, "Yes." She looked up to gaze once more at her sister's portrait. "Karen had a lot of influence on me, especially when it came to our parents. She really hated them. I'm only beginning to realize how much." She turned away from the picture, seeking shelter in his embrace. "Now I guess I'll have to rethink how I feel about them, but it won't be easy. Did you notice that everybody Karen and Steve swindled was just like them?"

"Yeah," he murmured. "Think it was some kind of twisted revenge?"

"Probably," she answered, stepping away from him. "When they left, it hurt her a lot more than me because Karen always protected me from the pain. She made sure I had the things a child usually gets from her parents—the things she didn't have anymore. Who knows? Without that, I might've ended up doing exactly what Karen did.''

"Bull." He took her hand as they started toward the hall. "You'd never do anything dishonest." Following her from the room, he closed the living room door firmly behind him. "Now, go get packed, or we'll miss breakfast at the farm."

She started to leave, but instead, turned back to face him, studying his features as though searching for the answer to some great mystery. Finally, she quietly asked, "What do you get out of all this, Daniel? After hiding the girls and me out at your family's farm, being a go-between for my parents and me, and helping me find a good attorney, what do *you* get—besides trouble?"

"Time," he replied, putting his heart on the line. "Sweetheart, you're going to need a lot of time to get over this and to learn to trust again. I want to be around when that happens."

Her gaze never wavered as a single tear slid down her cheek. "You don't have to wait for that," she said, her voice choked with emotion. "I trusted you the first time I ever heard your voice, and I should've relied more on my instinct. If I had, maybe I wouldn't have lost touch with what's really important. Through this whole nightmare, you never let me down. Not once. And it seems to me I'm the one with something to prove."

"Uh-uh," Daniel said softly, gently taking her face between his hands to tilt it toward his. "Not to me." Bending down, he brushed his lips lightly over hers, taking his time as he became reacquainted with her taste and touch.

And Rae returned his kiss. Closing her eyes, she leaned toward him, sliding her arms around his waist while they shared a sweet, exploratory caress that began to heal their bruised souls. When it ended, she sighed.

With her lips still so close he could almost feel them moving beneath his, she whispered, "I never stopped loving you, Daniel, not even during the worst of it."

Her words ran through him like an electrical charge, and everything inside him came alive again. It took all his self-control to keep from grabbing her and whirling her around the room, but after the trauma she had so recently experienced, she wouldn't be ready yet for that kind of enthusiasm. With all the restraint he could muster, he murmured, "I love you, too. That's what made being apart so hard." No matter how hard he tried, though, he couldn't suppress the smile he felt spread across his face or stop himself from adding, "And I'll tell you something else, Rae. Next time Kristen asks me to marry you, I'm gonna be ready with the right answer."

Her mouth twitched into the near smile he had seen so often on her niece's face, and he watched, intrigued, as it grew ever so slowly until it lit up her eyes.

"Just what makes you think I'm going to wait for Kris?" she answered softly, but with unmistakable commitment.

He chuckled, no longer able to contain his joy as he tightened his arms around her, drawing her as close as possible.

Rae still had some tough times ahead. They both did. But that didn't matter. They had each other and the girls, along with trust and love, and that would provide all the strength they'd need to secure their happiness forever.

SHARE THE FUN . . .
SHARE YOUR NEW-FOUND TREASURE!!

You don't want to let your new books out of your sight? That's okay. Your friends can get their own. Order below.

No. 149 VOICE IN THE DARK by Judy Whitten
Rae finally faced the man who saved her life. Now can she save his?

No. 10 FULL STEAM by Cassie Miles
Jonathan's a dreamer—Darcy is practical. An unlikely combo!

No. 11 BY THE BOOK by Christine Dorsey
Charlotte and Mac give parent-teacher conference a new meaning.

No. 12 BORN TO BE WILD by Kris Cassidy
Jenny shouldn't get close to Garrett. He'll leave too, won't he?

No. 18 RAINBOW WISHES by Jacqueline Case
Mason is looking for more from life. Evie may be his pot of gold!

No. 19 SUNDAY DRIVER by Valerie Kane
Carrie breaks through all Cam's defenses showing him how to love.

No. 21 THAT JAMES BOY by Lois Faye Dyer
Jesse believes in love at first sight. Will he convince Sarah?

No. 22 NEVER LET GO by Laura Phillips
Ryan has a big dilemma. Kelly is the answer to *all* his prayers.

No. 23 A PERFECT MATCH by Susan Combs
Ross can keep Emily safe but can he save himself from Emily?

No. 24 REMEMBER MY LOVE by Pamela Macaluso
Will Max ever remember the special love he and Deanna shared?

No. 25 LOVE WITH INTEREST by Darcy Rice
Stephanie & Elliot find $47,000,000 *plus* interest—true love!

No. 26 NEVER A BRIDE by Leanne Banks
The last thing Cassie wanted was a relationship. Joshua had other ideas.

No. 27 GOLDILOCKS by Judy Christenberry
David and Susan join forces and get tangled in their own web.

No. 28 SEASON OF THE HEART by Ann Hammond
Can Lane and Maggie's newfound feelings stand the test of time?

No. 31 WINGS OF LOVE by Linda Windsor
Mac & Kelly soar to new heights of ecstasy. Are they ready?

No. 32 SWEET LAND OF LIBERTY by Ellen Kelly
Brock has a secret and Liberty's freedom could be in serious jeopardy!

No. 33 A TOUCH OF LOVE by Patricia Hagan
Kelly seeks peace and quiet and finds paradise in Mike's arms.

No. 34 NO EASY TASK by Chloe Summers
Hunter is wary when Doone delivers a package that will change his life.

No. 35 DIAMOND ON ICE by Lacey Dancer
Diana could melt even the coldest of hearts. Jason hasn't a chance.

No. 36 DADDY'S GIRL by Janice Kaiser
Slade wants more than Andrea is willing to give. Who wins?

No. 37 ROSES by Caitlin Randall
It's an inside job & K.C. helps Brett find more than the thief!

No. 38 HEARTS COLLIDE by Ann Patrick
Matthew finds big trouble and it's spelled P-a-u-l-a.

No. 40 CATCH A RISING STAR by Laura Phillips
Justin is seeking fame; Beth helps him find something more important.

No. 41 SPIDER'S WEB by Allie Jordan
Silvia's quiet life explodes when Fletcher shows up on her doorstep.
